FALSE Love TRUE Love

A Novel

Gladys Krueger

Unless otherwise indicated, all Scripture quotations are taken from the King James Version of the Bible.

ISBN: 978-1-77069-422-4

Printed in Canada

Word Alive Press
131 Cordite Road, Winnipeg, MB R3W 1S1
www.wordalivepress.ca

Library and Archives Canada Cataloguing in Publication

Krueger, Gladys, 1937-
    False love, true love / Gladys Krueger.

ISBN 978-1-77069-422-4

    I. Title.

PS8621.R784F34 2011   C813'.6   C2011-907674-8

Dedication

To my husband, Wally, whose support
was greatly appreciated as I
wrote this novel.

Thanks for coming.
Gerri!

Gladys Krueger

Chapter 1

Jill took a deep breath and rubbed her eye. It always twitched when she was tired. But she felt ready for tomorrow. She thought of all the columns of job ads for teachers she had studied. Had she made the right choice to come to Brentville? It was near Saskatoon, where she had grown up and gone to school. Brentville was a one-room school with Grades One through Eight. What would the kids be like? What would their parents be like? Would she be able to cope?

She glanced around the room. The small desks were clustered around her own. Larger desks for the older students were separated to give them their own space. Pictures were on the wall, the school bell was ready on her desk, and she had her plan book open. She had printed the date firmly at the top of the first page—September 6, 1955.

It was eleven o'clock when she put on a sweater and went outside to stroll to her teacherage. The lights of Saskatoon flickered on the horizon. Dan was there. What was he doing tonight? She wondered briefly about calling, but quickly realized it was too late. He had been so helpful bringing her boxes out to the teacherage. Saskatoon was only fifteen miles away, but it might as well have been fifteen thousand miles without a car.

That would be her first major purchase when she started getting paychecks.

She thought of the past few weeks since meeting Dan. Actually, she thought of him often already! She could picture his wavy auburn hair, his muscular body, his deep blue eyes, and his thick eyebrows. She could hear his deep voice when he had called to ask for their first date. The memories already made her think of him romantically. Would he be her Prince Charming?

She shook her head. Tonight she had better think of Brentville and her adventure tomorrow. She had a feeling more time would be coming to think of Dan Fischer.

The sidewalk to her place led through a thick hedge. The thought of walking through it during the dark winter months made her uneasy. She'd check with Dan about having a better lock installed on her door.

When she reached her place, Jill sat on the porch steps to enjoy the night a little longer. Even at that hour, she could hear the sounds of a combine cutting hay in the nearby field. She sniffed the air to catch the scent of fresh mown hay. In the distance, she could see the bright lights of the combine. Was its driver the parent of one of her new students?

The stars were bright in the clear dark sky. She identified the Big Dipper and Orion. Someday she wanted to be able to recognize more constellations, but she loved looking at them even though she didn't know their names.

She was surprised to hear the honking of a late flock of geese. They flew raucously almost over her head. She could hear the swoosh of their wings as well as their calls. Were they encouraging each other to keep in line? It was always interesting to watch their disciplined V-shaped flight arrangement.

Well, she was going to lead the students who arrived in the morning. She hoped fervently that they would stay in line with her leading, but tonight she was tired and ready for bed. She got up, stretched, turned the knob, and walked into the place that would be home this next year.

Jill flipped on the lights as she went inside and surveyed her new home. It looked peaceful—just the way she wanted it. No thought of possible trouble disturbed her thoughts.

The kitchen was cheery. The school board had given her permission to move in the week before school started. They'd also given her permission to paint the kitchen. Bless her folks, who had helped her paint. She never had been able to wield a paintbrush without making a mess.

She had chosen a soft blue for the walls and sunshine yellow for the curtains and tablecloth. That was all she could afford before payday at the end of the month. But it brightened the room. When she got her first paycheck, she might get a few decorations, but the pictures she had brought from home helped.

Home. Mom and Dad. I don't think I thanked them for their help. I was so busy getting settled. Jill brightened. *I know what I'll do. I'll take them out for a celebration dinner at the end of the month when I get my first paycheck. I know they're proud of me. I was a good student.*

Ah, students. She was scared and excited to think about the morning. Jill fell asleep dreaming of students, of teaching, and of trying to find the misplaced—or hidden—chalk so she could write on the board.

Chapter 2

Jill got up early and dressed carefully. She wanted to make a good impression.

At the school, she watched the arriving children and made some mental notes. One little girl with reddish hair seemed to stand uncertainly away from the other children. She almost looked scared, leading Jill to wonder what was worrying her. Two boys were playing catch. A bigger boy with a brush-cut was whooping around and trying to catch the ball. He looked like trouble.

She glanced at the clock; it was time to ring the bell. She stood on the front step and firmly gripped the handle, giving the bell a good shake. As the clapper swung back and forth, the kids stopped their games and marched into the school.

When they were in their desks, Jill stood at the front, took a deep breath, and began.

"Good morning, class. My name is Miss Jackson. I hope you all had a good summer. I'm looking forward to a good school year with you, and also to getting to know each of you. I even hope to meet your parents."

So far, so good. They're quiet, sizing me up.

"Now, let's stand at attention for *Oh Canada*, and then recite the Lord's Prayer."

The class shuffled to their feet and stood respectfully. They all sang, although some were off-key.

"You can take your seats and get out crayons or pens. I'm going to give you each a paper and a pin. Write your names on the paper, and pin them on so I can learn your names faster."

Jill walked up and down the aisles, observing them as they wrote.

The shy girl with reddish hair wrote "Melissa Webber" on her tag and pinned it to her blouse. The brush-cut boy scrawled "Mike Orlick," pretended to prick himself as he pinned on his nametag, then slunk down in his seat. A well-dressed girl in third grade slowly printed "Honey Wheeler" on her tag and carefully pinned it to her new pinafore. Jill smiled as she watched a boy with an unevenly-buttoned shirt and a happy smile. His name was Randy Turner.

"Let's talk awhile about something special that happened during your summer holidays," she said. "First, I'll tell you something that was special for me. I went canoeing for the first time in my life. It was a little scary getting started and hoping the canoe wouldn't tip, but after we got going, I really enjoyed myself. Now, who wants to share next?"

Honey Wheeler raised her hand. "The most fun I had was when Mom took me shopping to buy new outfits for school." She smoothed her new pinafore and patted her curls.

"I made snares and caught gophers," Mike said. "They sure are pests. I drowned thirty of the ones I caught." He looked pleased with himself, but some of the girls shuddered at the thought of drowning gophers.

Randy said he got a bike from a friend and rode it for a mile one day.

Butch Taylor was the school janitor. He was the oldest in the class and seemed very mature. "Dad had me drive the tractor at our farm this summer," he announced.

Teresa McNeil pushed her glasses up her nose as she spoke. "My grandparents live in Medicine Hat. We went there for a few days. My grandma took me to the glass factory where they make fancy things out of glass."

Larry Thompkins, a boy in Grade Two, volunteered that he had helped his mom carry in water from the well.

After hearing from all the children who wanted to share, Jill had them take out their readers.

Soon it was time for recess. Jill was ready for a break, and so were the kids. She only had a moment to wonder whether Dan might come out tonight before she heard Randy ask Melissa to play catch. Honey heard, too. She patted her curls and commented, "Only boys play catch."

"Come on, Melissa," Randy said. "Don't mind that Miss Perfect. Let's go before recess is over." He walked Melissa to the door.

Honey made a face and followed.

After recess, Jill put them to work on different arithmetic lessons. It didn't seem like long before it was time to wash up and get out their lunches.

Soon the kids were either eating their lunch or trying to trade for someone else's. The smell of peeled bananas and oranges soon mingled with garlic.

"Phew," Honey coughed daintily. "Who has garlic in their sandwich?"

Jill sipped coffee from her thermos and made sure she was ready for the afternoon.

It sure would be nice if Dan called, she thought. *But that's a dumb idea. How can he call when we have no phone in the school?*

"It's time to clean up your lunch mess," Jill announced. "It's a bright, sunny day. Go outside and enjoy it until the bell goes."

Jill sighed and looked at her watch. *Ten more minutes until I ring the bell. I might as well go outside and join the kids.*

She got up, stretched, and went outside into the sunshine.

After lunch, the day went rather quickly. Jill read from *The Lion, the Witch, and the Wardrobe*, a book she thought they would all enjoy. Then they started lessons.

The day went on without major problems. Butch made a spelling mistake while writing on the blackboard. Some of the kids laughed, but Jill stopped them.

"We all make mistakes sometimes," she said. "How do you feel when people laugh at you?"

Four o'clock came.

"Goodnight, Miss Jackson." Honey stepped daintily out the door.

"Goodnight, Miss." Mike pretended to trip as he reached the step.

"Goodnight, Miss Jackson." Butch headed for his bike.

"Goodnight, Miss Jackson. I'm glad you are our teacher." Melissa stopped tentatively and Jill gave her a quick hug. Something about Melissa already tweaked her curiosity. She was such a sweet girl and yet she was withdrawn.

It was quiet when the last child left. Jill suddenly felt isolated. *I wish I could go bowling tonight. Or play tennis. But I've chosen to be here and I'm going to like the country life.*

She resolutely went back to her desk and set about planning her lessons for the next day.

Jill finished her plans, picked up her key, and locked the school. She walked slowly back to the teacherage savoring the late autumn warmth, the geese honking in flight, the colored leaves on the trees, and the hedge around the school grounds.

One especially bright red bush stood just outside her kitchen window. Its colors cheered her as she sat eating alone. Jill paused to pluck a leaf when she heard her phone ring. Filled with hope, she hurried inside.

Maybe that's Dan.

Chapter 3

∽

"Hello, Jill. We're back. How did the first day go?" Jill did her best to sound pleased that the phone call was from her mom. Of course, she would want to hear about Jill's day.

"Just great, Mom. I'll have my hands full, but I'm excited about it," Jill answered. "Tell me about your trip to the mountains."

Her mom gave a happy account of hiking, scenery, and good places to eat. "Your sister kept the house just great," Mom gushed in closing.

Good for Joanne. If she had set fire to the house, Mom would say she did a good job of calling the fire department, Jill thought sardonically as she said goodbye.

When she hung up, Jill planned a quick supper. Peanut butter and honey sandwiches sounded okay.

She had just cleared the table when the phone rang again. "Hello."

Her heart skipped as she heard Dan's voice.

"How would it be if I come out tonight?" Dan asked. "I'll bring stuff for hot dogs. You get everything ready for a fire. It's too nice a night to waste sitting inside."

"You got it. I'll get wood and kindling, but I'll wait until you get here to light the fire. I've got matches, but I'm no boy scout when it comes to lighting fires."

"Well, I wouldn't be coming for a wiener roast if you were a *boy* scout."

Jill could hear his smile.

"See you in about an hour," he said.

She scurried to tidy the kitchen. Next she laid out mugs and hot chocolate, mustard and catsup. Hurrying to her bathroom, she checked her face in the mirror. *Better pluck out some of those stray eyebrows.*

It was amazing how having something to look forward to gave her energy! Outside, she happily found dry twigs and branches for a fire.

Wonder if we'll need wienie sticks? Somehow, I think Dan will have that looked after.

She combed her hair and waited.

It didn't take long before she heard his pickup coming down the quiet road.

"Hey, Jill. How's it going?" he asked as he jumped out and brought the wienie sticks, wieners, and buns to the spot she had found for a fire. "You were right about one thing. You're not a boy scout."

Grinning, Dan knelt and carefully arranged the twigs to let the air blow through. Then he put the branches nearby. Finally, he got an axe from his pickup box and chopped some bigger branches. With a satisfied look, he brought out two old tree stumps for them to sit on.

"Who knows how long we'll be out here? Now we can enjoy ourselves when the evening cools off."

They both watched the kindling turn into a blaze.

"So," he said, "tell me about the day."

Jill recalled some highlights. "I think I have a potential troublemaker," she admitted. "There has to be a reason for his boisterous behavior, but I have no idea what it is." She sighed. "And there's one little girl, Melissa, who is so sweet, but seems to carry a weight on her little shoulders. I need to find out more about her."

"Remember, you can only do so much," Dan warned.

She nodded and asked how his day had been.

"I'll fill you in later," Dan said. "Let's check whether we can roast these yet. I'm hungry. How about you?"

Jill realized that hot dogs sounded great. One peanut butter sandwich hadn't lasted her long.

They each turned their wiener slowly on the stick while finding the best spot in the fire.

"Here's a good spot," Dan suggested. Jill moved closer. "Perfect."

Dan's smile made her heart skip.

The sky still had some late evening color. The setting sun's last rays glowed on the clouds in the sky. A cow mooed in the distance.

"Doesn't it seem like an occasional sound just accentuates the quiet here?" Jill asked, turning to look at Dan.

He bent his head, listening. "You're right. And it really is quiet here, peaceful… if you have someone to share it with. Have you met any neighbors yet? I don't like to think of you totally isolated here. Until you get a car, it would be nice to at least know someone close by."

She warmed at his apparent concern. "Actually, I think I'll walk down the road Sunday. There's a little country church. I'll see if I meet anyone there who seems friendly."

"I'd come and take you, but we have a family reunion this weekend. Mom and Dad count on me to drive them." Dan sighed. "Dad's reflexes aren't what they used to be."

"There's more hot chocolate in the thermos. Want some?"

"You bet. In a minute." Dan got up from his stump and put some more wood on the fire before he headed for the pickup and reached in for a blanket.

"Cools off in a hurry when the sun goes down, doesn't it?" He draped a blanket over her shoulders. "Can't have the teacher catching a cold the first week, can we?"

His arm lingered over her shoulder and Jill smiled up at him while handing him his mug of hot chocolate.

"I don't need to hog the whole blanket. It's big enough for two if you move your stump closer. I love to watch the colors change when the fire dies down to embers, but it doesn't give much warmth then."

"Agreed." Dan maneuvered his stump closer before pulling half the blanket over his shoulder. "This way we can keep our backs warm." Dan sipped his hot chocolate. "Hmmm. Tastes good. You're better at making hot chocolate than fires."

They both laughed.

The stars came out brightly.

"When we were kids, we'd look at different bright stars at night and name them after ourselves," Jill admitted. "We used to visit our cousins on the farm where we could really see the stars at night. Good memories."

"Time for new memories," Dan said, looking at Jill. "I think this firepit needs a name. How about Jill's Cookhouse?" He smiled.

The embers died, the evening cooled, and Dan got up and stretched.

"Work for both of us tomorrow. I'll get water to douse the fire and say goodnight. It's been a special evening."

Jill agreed and helped make sure the fire was out.

They walked the path to the teacherage and Dan leaned over to kiss her goodnight. Jill happily responded.

Thoughts of Dan totally eclipsed any concerns about the students she would see in the morning.

Chapter 4

Morning came too soon. Jill stretched before getting up to face the day.

My second day as a teacher. She felt that moment of fear, took a deep breath, and marched to the school. There were no kids in sight yet, so she sat at her desk reviewing her plans for the day. Soon she could hear voices and saw that the playground was starting to fill.

Honey Wheeler patted her hair before prancing by the boys playing ball. Melissa Webber sat alone on a swing, watching the other kids. Randy Turner still hadn't finished tucking in his shirt, but she smiled as he waved eagerly at a newcomer and almost tripped running to meet him.

Soon it was time to ring the bell. *This is fun. How hard can I whack this thing?* She shook it vigorously, enjoying the ring of the clapper on the metal.

"Do you like ringing the bell?"

Jill looked down to find Teresa staring up at her.

"Can I try?" Teresa asked hopefully.

"Remind me at recess," Jill promised. "I'll let you try then."

Teresa nodded and smiled.

Jill met the students coming in. "Good morning, Randy. Hello, Melissa."

Melissa responded with a shy smile.

Wherever possible, she called them by name. As the students filed in, she watched them carefully for clues as to what to expect. Mike Orlick managed to fake a stumble on the stair and clutched roughly at Randy. Randy informed her in passing that Butch had to stay home and help his dad hay.

"I'm impressed how well you stand at attention," Jill commented as the children sat down after singing *Oh Canada*. "It shows we really are proud of our country. Now, take out your arithmetic books and we'll get going."

Jill assigned work and walked up the aisle.

Whew, she thought, pausing at Larry Thompkin's desk. *He needs a bath. Don't they have running water?*

She heard Marie Stollery stumble as she came back from the pencil sharpener. "You did that on purpose," Marie said, glaring at Mike.

"Sorry," he smirked. "You need to watch where you're going."

Jill sighed. She needed to know when to reprimand and when to ignore. She'd keep Mike in at recess for a few minutes; he could help her move her desk, and then she could talk to him alone. Maybe she would get some idea why he was so cocky.

"The leaves are beautiful now," she told the students before dismissing them for lunch. "Gather some over the noon hour. We'll press them and use them for art later."

They all hurried outside to eat their lunch in the September sunshine.

It sure would be nice to have someone to talk to. Guess I'll get used to a quiet lunch. I'll go outside later and talk to the kids.

Jill opened her lunch at her desk.

I wonder how Dan's day is going. What a difference there is between him and Gordon Curtiss!

She recalled Gordon coming out of Mrs. Brewer's house next door to her folks. He'd jerked his thumb at Mrs. Brewer's door. "My mom sent me to bring the old lady some baking."

"She's a sweet lady," Jill had defended.

"Also old," Gordon had added while leering at Jill. She'd gone inside her parents' home to avoid him. Later she had gone to check on Mrs. Brewer to make sure she was okay.

"I heard you had some company," she remembered saying.

Mrs. Brewer had supplied Gordon's name, then said, "He needs some decent friends. Life with his dad has been rough."

Jill didn't comment. However, she certainly had an answer in mind. "I'd like a husband someday, but not a psych patient."

Just two weeks ago, I was home visiting a neighbor. Well, life has changed.

She got up from her desk, stretched, and strolled outside. Two girls were turning the rope while another skipped.

"Can I take one end?" Jill offered. One girl happily offered her the end of the rope and soon two girls were skipping and chanting.

"Wanna try?" Marie asked her, offering to turn the rope.

Jill laughed and ran in to skip with Sharon Martins. They chanted a skipping verse, then Jill ran out to turn the rope again. She was pleased she could still run in and out without tangling the rope.

She let Teresa ring the bell for class. The afternoon went quickly as the children did their lessons and pressed the leaves they had gathered.

It was almost four o'clock when Jill became aware of someone peeking in a window. The kids who saw the face were nervous. Suddenly, the "someone" clomped up the stairs and walked in.

16

It was Gordon. Jill had hoped he didn't know where she taught.

"Just thought I could sit in a back seat and learn something," Gordon smirked while lounging into the only empty desk.

"Teacher's got a boyfriend," she heard a few loud whispers. Obviously Gordon heard them, too, as he folded his arms and watched. She could feel him eyeing her.

Settling the class, she spoke in what she hoped was an authoritative voice.

"Mr. Curtiss, visitors aren't allowed to drop in during class. I'll have to ask you to leave."

Would he? The students were watching.

Gordon pulled himself out of the desk and headed to the door. Jill breathed a sigh of relief, then shuddered as he slammed the door on his way out.

"Watch out for people with tempers," she advised the children. "If your parents ever want to come, they are welcome. Just have them let me know first so we expect them."

It was four o'clock now, but Jill made sure Gordon's truck was gone before she dismissed the students.

By six, she had finished her plans for the next day, so she headed home to an empty house, wondering what she would do all evening. Would Gordon return later? She fervently hoped not. Would Dan call? That was a much more inviting prospect.

She opened her door, paused, and headed for the jar of peanut butter.

Chapter 5

J ill was glad when Friday arrived, but it had been a good week nonetheless. Dan's visit and his phone calls were a highlight. Tonight he would be on his way to the family reunion.

She cringed as she thought of Gordon's unwelcome visit. Thankfully, he hadn't pulled that stunt again—at least not this week.

Mrs. Brewer had mentioned Gordon's miserable father, but that wasn't enough to excuse his rude behavior, was it? His mother must be nice to be a friend of Mrs. Brewer. Jill would enjoy talking to Mrs. Brewer the next time she was home for a visit, since Mrs. Brewer was a retired teacher. She could ask for some advice on how to deal with Melissa's occasional withdrawals and Mike's sly pestering of other students.

Jill finished her lesson plans, made copies of some worksheets on the Ditto machine, and somewhat reluctantly headed down the path. The thought of a lonely supper didn't whet her appetite.

In the kitchen, she found some celery to cut and stuff with cheese, a box of macaroni and cheese, an apple, and some milk that was still fresh.

It was still early when she finished supper. Maybe she could walk down the road and see some neighbors? Jill found her cardigan sweater and slipped it on before starting out. She wouldn't need to lock her door here in the country.

Savoring the colored leaves still hanging on bushes and trees, she picked a couple to twirl between her fingers while she walked. A flock of geese flew almost over her head. She wondered idly if they were honking because they were glad to be going south, or if they were just keeping up their birdie spirits. Jill listened as the honking faded into the distance.

She sniffed at the sweet scent of clover growing along the road. It was a welcome scent, reminding her that summer was lingering. But autumn was well underway. She heard a combine in the next field and saw the truck alongside it catching the precious grain.

"Hello. Out for an evening walk?"

Jill jumped and turned toward the voice. A woman she had never seen before was standing along the side of the road, watching her.

"Oh, hello," Jill answered. "It's too nice a night to stay in. I love to be outdoors. By the way, I'm Jill Jackson, the new teacher. I came out for a stroll and hoped I might meet a neighbor or two."

"It's great to have you down the road," the woman said. "It'll be good to have a friendly neighbor. I'm Linda Martins. Do you want to stop and visit?"

Linda Martins? This must be Sharon's mother.

"I'd love to. I'm not used to a weekend with nothing to do, and I always love to visit with a friend."

Jill walked through the gate Linda had opened.

"What a beautiful garden!" Jill exclaimed.

The carrot tops were still green, some beans were climbing on their trellis, and a few sweet peas still blossomed. Everywhere was the evidence of care. No weeds… just straight garden rows.

"You must spend a lot of time here," Jill commented.

"Well, I enjoy it," Linda said. "It keeps my mind on something beautiful."

Linda stooped to pull some carrots. She shook the dirt off them before handing them to Jill.

"Here," she said. "I'll bet you'd like some fresh carrots. And how about a few sweet peas to brighten your kitchen?"

Jill looked up just in time to see Sharon coming down the lane toward them. The girl rubbed her eyes and pushed a braid back over her shoulder.

"Oh, Miss Jackson!" Sharon said. "I didn't know you were here."

Jill smiled. "Hello, Sharon. I was just walking down the road and your mom invited me in for a visit. Do you help her in the garden?"

"Well, I help her weed. But not too early in spring because I still can't tell the young weeds from the young plants." Sharon paused. "If you want to help next spring, I'll bet Mom would let you."

Linda laughed. "Miss Jackson will be busy marking papers and planning lessons. She won't have time for our garden."

Sharon's face fell. "Well, if you have time, you could come. It would be nice to have you here."

"That is a very kind offer," Jill replied, "and I just might take you up on it. I get tired sitting at the desk all day."

"Yeah. I know what you mean." Sharon sighed. "Especially at the start of school when you still think about being outside all day."

Jill smiled.

"Want a cup of tea?" Linda asked. "I just baked some cookies and we need help eating them."

Jill laughed. "I'd be glad to help my new neighbor with that problem!"

They both chuckled and walked inside.

Before long, twilight was deepening.

"Soon we'll be at equinox," Jill said with a sigh. "I'll miss the long hours of summer light, and I know I'll be hesitant to go out walking alone when it's dark outside.

"That reminds me," Linda said. "Let's trade phone numbers. When it's dark early, I can drive up to your place, if you don't mind. Or I can pick you up and bring you here."

"Oh, Linda, I was hoping so much to find a friend nearby. I'd welcome you anytime. I won't be able to serve you cookies as good as these, but I can brew tea."

They both laughed.

"It's getting dark and I'd better head home." Jill picked up her cup and saucer and put them in the sink. "Thanks again for everything."

Linda walked her to the door.

"Goodbye, teacher," Sharon said, waving.

"See you Monday." Jill smiled, then looked at Linda. "I'm looking forward to being friends."

She waved as she walked out the door.

What a lovely surprise in what I thought would be a boring evening. Maybe her husband was out combining. Anyway, I'll certainly be happy having Linda as a friend.

Jill headed up her driveway, pausing to look up at the stars and savor the autumn air. With a light heart, she opened her door and walked inside.

Chapter 6

Stepping into her kitchen, Jill switched on the light. Out of habit, she pulled down the blinds. *I know most country folk leave their blinds up, but I still feel more secure with them down.* She checked that the bottom of each blind touched the windowsill and then went into her bedroom.

She smiled to herself as she hung up her clothes after taking them off.

Well, this is a change for the better. I'm going to keep a tidy room.

Jill shrugged into a warm housecoat and headed back to the kitchen. *Should I bake something? But I didn't bring a cookbook. Should I make a grocery list? It would need to be short, at least until payday. Should I phone the folks and see what they're doing?*

She picked up the phone and dialed. At least Saskatoon wasn't long distance for phone calls, even if it felt like long distance without a car to go to town.

"Hello," her sister answered.

Her heart sank a little at the sound of Joanne's voice.

"Hi, Joanne." Jill rummaged through her mind, trying to make conversation. "How did your week go? Anything new at the clothes department?"

"Well, I got a beautiful new cardigan sweater, if that's what you mean," Joanne answered. "When you get a paycheck, maybe you can come in and find something new for your closet." Jill felt the intended sting. Joanne had lots of lovely clothes, but Jill had spent her money on school, not on clothes.

"How are things with you?" Joanne asked. "Feeling lonely on the quiet weekend?"

"Well, I had a nice visit with a new neighbor."

"I thought you had a new boyfriend. Didn't he show up?"

Jill didn't rise to the bait. Joanne didn't need to know that it would be days before Dan came, *if* he came at all. "Are the folks home?"

"Nope. Went out visiting. And I'm meeting friends soon, so I'll need to sign off."

"Sure. Well, have fun. Tell the folks I called."

"Yes. And you have fun there in the country."

Jill hung up. *Why does Joanne always seem to antagonize me? What pulls us apart? And why does Mom always favor Joanne?*

Just then, the phone rang.

"Hey, Miss Priss. How did the week go?"

Jill stiffened at the sound of Gordon's voice. "Pretty well, thanks. I'm going to like it here."

"Want me to come and rescue you this weekend? We could go to the A&W for a hamburger tomorrow."

Jill took a deep breath. *It sounds appealing, but with Gordon? I'm not that desperate yet.*

"Well, that's a nice offer, but I need to plan lessons here. Besides, Mom and Dad are coming out tomorrow," she added. *I'll be surprised if they don't show up.*

"Excuses, excuses. Why don't you just say you think you're too good to go out with me?"

She heard Gordon's phone slam down. She carefully hung up her own.

I'm not saying I'm too good for him. He just irks me. I'm sorry his dad is mean, but I can't change that. I hope he doesn't call again. He scares me a little.

She wandered into her small living room and picked up a photo album. Some of the pictures were coming loose. Jill made a mental note to pick up some photo corners when she got her paycheck—and to take a picture of Dan for her album.

As she flipped the pages, she remembered family events. Decorating the Christmas tree. Turkey dinner with the aunts, uncles, and cousins. A holiday at Waskesiu Lake. Catching her first fish. She smiled, remembering that event. *I was so afraid he'd come off the hook before I landed him. I was so proud. Now I see it really was a small fish.*

She turned the pages slowly. A Grade Five class picture caught her eye. Mom had insisted on rebraiding her hair for the afternoon picture. She did look neat in the picture. Jill looked carefully. Most of the kids no longer had names in her memory.

I should take a picture of my first school and the kids here. We'll put the names on, too.

When it was ten o'clock, Jill stretched and went to bed.

It was too early to be in bed, though. Jill turned and shifted in bed, fluffed her pillow, and tried to think of beautiful and restful scenes. After a restless hour, she heard the coyotes start to yip.

Drat, those coyotes. I wonder how close they are?

Jill got up and peered out her window. The moon was bright enough to make shadows on the ground.

Except for those coyotes howling, it's so quiet. No cars driving by. No sirens. No people talking on the street. Not a coyote in sight here. No one but me in the house. I see the lights of Saskatoon on the horizon—the lights of Saskatoon on the horizon across fifteen miles of dark prairie.

Jill glanced at the clock. Only eleven. She put her housecoat back on and decided to make a cup of tea and read. She was wide awake. If she was tired in the morning, she could sleep in.

I wonder how Dan is enjoying the reunion? How many times have we been together now? Only four? His kisses are so tender.

Jill daydreamed as she poured water into her teapot. It overflowed.

Not my night, she thought. She wiped up the puddle of water, sighed, poured her cup of tea, and sat down in her easy chair with a book.

But she couldn't read, either. *What's wrong with me? I can't sleep. Can't read. I can only hear coyotes howling and think of how I'll handle ten kids in eight grades. My mind is full! I'm scared of Gordon, I can't relate to my sister, and I'm concerned about Melissa. What is her family like?*

Finally she got up, checked that she had locked the door, and headed back to bed. Everything could wait until tomorrow.

When she heard the phone ring, she almost tripped on her housecoat as she hurried to answer.

Chapter 7

Jill's stomach seized up. It was after midnight. Was something wrong at home? Surely Gordon wouldn't be calling to pester her.

Tentatively, she lifted the receiver. "Hello?"

"Hi there," a deep voice answered. "What are you doing up this late?"

"Dan?" she asked timidly. "Is this Dan?"

Dan chuckled. "Who'd ya expect? The bogeyman?"

"Not a bogeyman. But I'm glad it's you. How was the drive? Did your folks manage okay?"

"The drive was long and tiring, but we all made it. Stopped along the way for the folks to stretch. Got here to face about a hundred people at the reunion. My hand is sore from shaking everyone's hands. My head is full of names and trying to figure out where we all fit. I needed some quiet time and I thought of all the peace in the country. So I called you. Hope you don't mind. I know it's late there. Later still here." He chuckled again.

"Well, I'm glad you called. It was so quiet here this evening that the only thing I could hear was the coyotes. I tried reading, but I couldn't concentrate, so I'm up roaming. I looked out the window, but couldn't see where the coyote pack was howling. They sounded close, though."

"Anything new besides coyotes? Don't you have a radio so you can hear real music?"

"No radio yet. But I'll survive awhile without it. Anyway, I had a great surprise this evening. I went for a stroll and met someone. It was the mother of one of my kids. She's just up the road from here. She asked me in for a visit and tea, so it looks like I'll have a friend close by. She's a gardener and gave me a bunch of fresh carrots. They taste so much better than store-bought ones. And she likes to talk, not just sit."

"Hey, I'm relieved you've already found someone close by," Dan said. "Does she have a phone so you can call if you ever need quick help?"

"Yup. Already have her number. But I'm hoping I don't have to use it to get help. Looks pretty calm out here."

Except for Gordon. He scares me a little.

"Oh, brother. Someone else wants the phone," he said. "We have to get in line to use it! Anyway, take care. I'll call you when we get back Monday."

"Great. Enjoy the weekend. Massage your sore hand and full brain!"

They both laughed and said goodnight.

Long distance. He called long distance. That must mean he cares, if he would pay to call long distance. He waited in line just to call me. Hooray! Ohhh, Monday, hurry up and come. Gordon, please don't call again. I'll call the folks in the morning and see if they want to come out tomorrow afternoon… Gordon just might drive out to check on me. Oh, I'm crazy to worry about him. Time to go to bed and stay there until morning.

Tomorrow will be my first Saturday here. What can I do to make it special?

Chapter 8

Jill licked the last of the cereal off her spoon and stirred her coffee. *Gorgeous day. Mom seemed pleased that I asked them to come out this afternoon. That makes the afternoon special and leaves morning and evening open for a plan.*

The phone rang—a welcome interruption.

"Morning," Jill chirped.

"Hi, Jill, this is Linda. Don't want to pester, but I'm driving to Saskatoon for groceries and wondered if there's anything you need or if you'd like to come in with Sharon and me."

"Like to?" Jill laughed. "I'd love to. It's a splendid day for a drive, even if it's just to Saskatoon. When do you want to leave?"

"Well, I should have phoned sooner. Is ten minutes too soon?"

"I'll be ready in nine, if you want."

Jill was at the door when Linda turned into the yard. Sharon sat demurely in the back seat pulling on one of her braids.

The warm sun shone in through the car windows. The leaves still on the trees were colorful in the sunshine. Goldenrod still bloomed in the ditches. Farmers were making use of the sunshine to finish getting in their crops.

"What a lovely day," Jill breathed.

"Yes. Howard is in the field. He hopes to finish this weekend. He's been able to hire some help, so I don't have to be in the field driving the truck. I'm free as a bird to go shopping."

It didn't take long to get to the market and find a place to park.

"Usually I don't shop on Saturdays," Linda explained. "Too many people."

They sauntered through the door.

"You go ahead," Jill said. "Take your time. I just need a few things, so I'll wait here at the door when I finish."

Jill started looking for bread. As she walked up the aisles, she smelled the bakery. Fresh cinnamon buns would be wonderful, but those sorts of treats would have to wait.

Bread, milk, some hamburger, and dry beans should tide me over. It's going to feel like a long time until that first paycheck.

Eyes searching for the till, she didn't notice the man until he bumped into her.

"Watch where you're going, Miss Priss," he growled.

She looked up into the stormy eyes of Gordon Curtiss.

"Sorry, Gordon. I didn't see you. I was looking for the checkout."

"Yeah. Thought your folks were coming out. How did you get here without a car?"

"They're coming this afternoon," Jill said. "And a friend brought me to get groceries."

"They better be coming. I intend to watch and see if you're lying to me. I have a hard time with people lying."

Gordon leaned toward her, but Jill held her groceries between them.

"I've never been accused of lying and won't start now," Jill answered with more assurance than she felt. "I need to pay for these before we leave, so please, excuse me."

29

"Right, Miss Priss."

Gordon affected a bow with a sweep of his arm, which nearly scattered her groceries. Jill saw the nearest checkout and got into line.

She fumbled in her purse to find some cash. In her haste, she dropped two quarters which seemed to ring and bounce on the floor. Feeling conscious of people turning, she bent hurriedly to retrieve them, paid for her groceries, and headed toward the door. She could feel her cheeks turning beet red.

It was a relief to arrive at the door to wait for Linda and Sharon.

Usually she could enjoy watching people. She would concentrate on other customers now to get her mind off her encounter with Gordon. Had he left, or would he show up and embarrass her in front of Linda and Sharon? Jill focused on the other customers.

There was an elderly man helping his wife, who was using a cane. A woman carrying a baby in one arm was trying to hang onto some bread and milk with her other arm. A middle-aged couple was holding hands and looked like they were worried about something. Jill glanced around and then realized that Linda and Sharon had arrived with their groceries.

"Ready?" Linda asked.

"Ready!" Jill answered gratefully.

How could Gordon be here at the same time as we are? He sounded threatening. Will he really come out and watch for my folks? Is he truly dangerous or just scary and rude?

Jill eased into the car.

"Find everything?" she asked Linda.

"All but the creamy honey. How about you?" Linda glanced at the scant grocery bag on Jill's lap.

"Oh yes. I didn't need much."

Jill wondered whether to share with Linda her concern over Gordon. After all, he had walked into the school unannounced and upset the kids as well as her. She decided to talk to Linda the first chance she had, when they were alone.

Chapter 9

Jill put the hamburger in the meat drawer and the milk on a nearly empty shelf in the small kitchen fridge. The bread and beans fit easily into a cupboard.

I'm sure glad for those carrots from Linda. Maybe I'll lose some weight this month. I won't be spending more than necessary on groceries!

She spread some peanut butter and honey on a slice of brown bread and sat down to have lunch and wait for her folks.

Hearing a vehicle on the road, she jumped up to check. No. It was neither her folks or Gordon. The Webbers lived on down the road. Maybe it was Melissa's dad.

Jill forced herself to read. Having so much spare time was foreign to her. She was used to assignment and exam deadlines, to meeting friends for tennis or bowling or roller skating—or just visiting. Most of her classmates had left since graduation for other places, but now that she was settled she needed to touch base with those who were still in town.

Suddenly uneasy, she glanced out the window. Sure enough, Gordon's truck was parked down the road. The knot in her stomach relaxed as she saw dust in the distance and realized it was her folks. Jill chuckled with relief. When had she ever been so glad to see them arrive?

Jill threw open the door.

"I'm so glad you could come out," she gushed. "Isn't it a lovely day? Look at this bush of red leaves. I just love looking at it while I eat."

Katie Jackson came in with her arms full. "Oh, your place looks so cozy. Here, I brought some cake I made. We can have it with our tea. And could you use some leftover stew? I made a big batch and we can't eat it all."

"Thanks, Mom. I miss your cooking. I'm not taking much time for cooking while I get used to planning lessons and getting to know the kids."

"Met any parents yet?" Tom Jackson asked from the easy chair where he had settled himself. "We're a little nervous about you being alone out here."

"Yes, Dad. I met a mother just down the road. I'll meet more soon, I hope. You know how I love having company."

She glanced out the window toward the road. The truck with the unwelcome company was gone.

"Ready for tea? I can't wait to try Mom's cake." Jill enjoyed her mom's pleased expression as she put the kettle on to boil. "We'll use my pretty teacups. This is your first visit without having to help me unpack. I want it to be special."

Jill hurried outside, picked a branch of colored leaves, then came back inside and laid them on the table as a centerpiece.

"Come and dine," she said with a laugh as she poured the tea and sliced cake.

They each settled around the table.

"I even have some napkins." Jill proudly unfolded them, then passed the cake to her folks before taking a piece herself.

"Good cake, Mom. I love the creamy icing on carrot cake. Maybe someday I could learn how to make this myself."

Maybe Dan would like this. I might have him over for dinner and dessert someday.

"I'd love to help you," her mom said. "Next time you're home for a weekend, we could make one."

"I'm not sure when I'll get in without a car," Jill said, "but we'll plan on baking when I get there. So, what's new? Did you bring any pictures of your trip?"

Her mother pulled out an envelope. "Well, I don't want to bore you, but I did bring some pictures. They're mainly scenery, but we are in a few of them."

Jill took the offered envelope, pulled out the pictures, and started looking through them.

"This is a good one of you both. Can I borrow the negative? I'd like to make a print to put up here—start a home gallery, you know."

"Well, sure," her mom said. "I should have put the negatives in. I'll try to remember next time I see you."

Dad reached for another piece of cake.

"Watch that tummy," Mom warned.

Dad just grinned and pushed half the piece into his mouth. "Can't watch my tummy unless it gets to where I can see it," he teased with his mouth full.

"Heard any good jokes lately?" Dad asked. "I heard a good one at the store the other day, but I forget the punchline. Guess I'm slipping a little. I was famous for my good jokes." He sighed. "I'd better brush up. A girl living alone needs a few jokes to cheer her."

"Well, so far I have to settle for the kids' jokes. 'Knock, knock…' I hear those all the time on the playground. Not that they compare with the jokes you used to tell at the supper table."

Jill smiled, remembering. Some of the jokes had been corny, others had surprise endings, but Dad always timed the punchline for the maximum humor.

"How's the money holding out?" Dad looked at Jill over his glasses. "Got enough to hold you until payday? You know, we'd loan you something to tide you over if you needed it."

Dear Dad. I should know that he's kept books long enough to know it can be tight between paychecks. I won't try to fool him—but I want to start off clear.

"Thanks, Dad—and Mom. I appreciate the offer. If I'm stuck, I'll come to you, but I want to try to manage."

"Kind of thought you'd say that. Just wanted to make sure." Dad wiped his glasses on his hankie. "Don't you have a meeting tonight, Katie?"

"Oh my goodness, yes," Jill's mom said. "It starts at six-thirty. I'm always a little early for it. Tonight, we plan a Christmas dinner for the seniors at the lodge. I guess we'd getter get going."

Mom hopped up from the table and found her purse.

"Thanks, Jill," she said. "I'll just leave the rest of the cake with the stew."

Dad took a little longer getting up. Jill noticed he limped a little as he came to her, put his arm around her, and gently said, "We're both proud of you, my girl."

Mom nodded.

Jill watched as Mom took Dad's arm and they walked back to the car.

Thank goodness they came. They are special. Now, supper is settled. Stew, milk, and bread—bread without peanut butter and honey. Good deal. After supper, I'll walk awhile in the other direction.

It's still early. I wonder if Wilma's home? I haven't seen or heard from her since we left school, but I'm sure she's still in Saskatoon. I think I'll give her a call and find out what she's doing and where she's working.

Jill picked up the receiver and dialed.

"Hey, Wilma. This is Jill. Just wondering how you're doing and what's up."

"Jill? So glad you called. I'm doing great. I just got a job in the office of Hudson's Bay. I've been wondering where you ended up teaching. I don't think you're here in Saskatoon."

"You're right. I'm about fifteen miles out of town in a one-room, eight-grade school. I think I'll like it. It's hard work, but the kids seem manageable. I'm not strong at discipline, so I need to be careful. Are you still dating Harvey?"

Wilma laughed. "Nope. Harvey was too tame. I've met a guy named Gordon who is a challenge, but I think he has potential. He's a little unpredictable, but he's exciting."

Jill swallowed. "What's his last name?"

"Curtiss. My mom knows his mom. Says she's a nice lady. I don't know anything about his dad."

Jill wondered what to say. "Well, I hope things work out for you. Just remember it's Gordon you're dating and not his mom. I've heard of unpredictable turning unmanageable, so take your time."

Wilma laughed. "Have you got anyone calling these days?"

Jill smiled as she thought of Dan. Dan was polite, thoughtful, and fun.

"Well, I've met someone I like. Time will tell what happens."

"I've got a car now," Wilma said. "How would it be if I drive out sometime? Maybe Gordon would come with me."

This is too much. How do I get out of this one?

"Right now, the days are pretty full getting started here. But we'll keep in touch. It must be nice to have a car. Gives you so much independence. I'm sure hoping to get one—the sooner the better."

"Good luck. I have to go now. Gordon is honking for me to come out."

Honking for her? His mom may be nice, but she sure didn't teach him any manners. It didn't take him long to get from our road to her place.

Jill hung up the phone. She didn't know Wilma well, but it was apparent that Wilma was setting herself up to know Gordon in ways she didn't anticipate.

Chapter 10

J ill cleared up supper and started walking north along the gravel road. A sign warned that there was no exit. Before long, she crossed a small bridge and noticed a house at the end of the road.

That must be the Webber house. Looks a little rundown from here. I think I'll turn around.

Just then, a car came out of the Webber driveway. Raising dust, the driver was obviously in a hurry. He slowed as he came near Jill.

Rolling down his window, he enquired politely. "Are you lost, miss?"

Jill noticed his black eyes and his muscular arms on the steering wheel. He wore a light jacket which didn't quite cover the suspenders on his plaid flannel shirt.

"No, I'm just out for a walk."

"This is a dead-end road, miss. Just leads to some private property."

Jill caught the word "private." It was apparent that she wasn't welcome to roam in this direction.

"Actually, I was just turning around when I saw you coming. I thought I'd better wait until you passed to make sure I was out of your way. Pedestrian safety, you know." Jill laughed a little nervously.

"Have a nice evening." The man touched his cap, rolled up his window, and drove away.

Well, it seems I've met Steve Webber, Melissa's dad. Polite, but a little overpowering. Maybe that's why Melissa seems so shy and withdrawn.

Jill turned and strolled slowly back toward the teacherage.

Tonight's walk wasn't nearly as pleasant as last night's. Can't win them all.

Tomorrow she'd walk south again and visit the chapel she had seen.

She reached her door, flipped on a light, pulled the blinds, put on the kettle for tea, and wondered idly what Dan was doing.

&

Jill woke to see sunshine streaming in around the edges of her bedroom blinds. *Ahhhh, a new day… plus a new adventure.*

She stretched and rolled out of bed. Slipping into a housecoat, she made coffee and toast and poured some cereal into a bowl.

Only nine o'clock. Likely church starts at eleven, so I have lots of time. A leisurely soak in the tub would be nice. I'll read while I soak. What luxury! No Joanne pounding on the door wanting in to put on her makeup.

Jill was ready to step out the door by ten-thirty. She checked herself in the mirror.

I'm glad I bought this little hat. The blue goes with my eyes and the hat covers my cowlick. Not that I'm any fashion model like Joanne, but

I want to look my best—first impressions count. I don't want the people I meet to think the new teacher is a slob. Good thing this purse is fairly big. I'll just slide my heels in and walk in running shoes.

Jill decided to lock her door when she left.

At the church door, she switched to her good shoes and stuffed her runners into her purse. With a quick check to make sure the seams on her nylons were straight, she opened the door and walked inside.

A friendly usher welcomed her and offered to show her to a seat.

"I'd like to sit near the back, if you don't mind," she whispered.

The usher nodded and smiled.

She slipped into her seat and looked around. The church wasn't large. She felt cozy in it. The pulpit was plain, with a small stained-glass window behind it. A familiar picture of Jesus with children around him hung on a side wall near the front of the sanctuary.

Jill turned her attention to the congregation. She guessed that most of them were farmers. A few seniors sat scattered among the young families. Some seniors held a grandchild in their laps.

She spied Linda.

That must be her husband with her. He has a kind expression. I'll try to talk to them after the service.

The leader announced the first hymn. Jill found a hymnbook and was glad to see that the hymn was familiar.

The preacher didn't look much older than Jill. He had a strong voice and was easy to listen to. However, Jill soon found herself looking around and daydreaming about Dan.

She must have lost track of time, because it was a surprise when the closing hymn was announced. With a little pang of guilt, she found the page and joined in singing.

As soon as the benediction was announced, she heard a greeting.

"Good morning, Miss Jackson."

Jill turned and saw Sharon Martins behind her. She was holding a braid in each hand, pulling them over her shoulder.

"Hello, Sharon. How are you? I see you have French braids today. Did your mom do them for you?"

Sharon nodded happily.

"Mom and Dad are over there," she said, pointing across the church. "I was looking around during church and I saw you. I told Mom I was coming over."

Sharon pushed her braids back and looked expectantly for her mother to arrive. She looked a little disappointed when the pastor and his wife came to greet Jill.

"Glad to have you here this morning," the pastor said. "I'm Pastor Gilmore and this is my wife, Helen. Welcome."

Jill introduced herself while noting the Gilmores. The pastor stood straight and was about six feet tall. Helen looked like fun. Her eyes sparkled behind her glasses—glasses which she kept pushing up the bridge of her nose. Her dress was colorful, but quite plain. Jill decided immediately she would like to know this woman better.

She was surprised when she heard Helen's offer.

"We usually take someone home with us for lunch… nothing fancy. Just a chance to get acquainted. We're quite new here. Anyway, we'd love to have you come if you're free."

"What a lovely offer," Jill said. "I'm new here, too, and getting acquainted. I'd enjoy coming."

What a nice surprise. And I surprised myself by accepting!

Jill turned, but it seemed that Sharon and her folks had left. She would meet Howard Martins another time.

Most of the people had left, so Helen invited Jill to follow her to the house behind the church. It was quite hidden from the road. Jill tried to walk up the lane in her heels, lamenting that the dust would sift into the open toes of her shoes. However, she was too proud to pull out her walking shoes for the short distance.

"Here's home," Helen announced. "We've only been here three months. I'm still deciding where to put things. And I'd like to either paint or paper this place, but I would have to ask the church board."

Jill chuckled. "I know what you mean. I had to ask the school board for permission to paint the teacherage. I'm pleased with the colors now, but I want some pictures and curtains—maybe a small rug to make it more homey. I'll have to spread out my wish list between paychecks, but anticipation is half the fun."

Helen started lunch and Jill offered to help.

"Here, you can put on the salad." Helen produced a lemon Jello salad with pineapple chunks. "That will have to do for dessert today—along with some cookies."

"Looks good to me. My mom always has Jello for a standby."

"Then this should make you feel at home."

Helen smiled and Jill realized that she already felt at home with her.

"The knives and forks are in that drawer," Helen said, nodding in the direction of the needed cutlery.

Jill was happy to set the table. It gave her something to do while they visited.

"Lunch ready?" a baritone voice asked. Jill turned to see the pastor walk into the kitchen. "Sorry, I'm slow. One couple wanted to talk to me."

"Everything okay?" Helen wondered.

"They're just planning a trip and letting us know they'll be gone a few weeks," he assured her. "That's nice. They didn't want me to think they'd dropped out."

"Well, lunch is ready."

Helen ladled soup into their bowls and put out fresh homemade bread and sliced cheese.

Jill waited while Rev. Gilmore said grace. It was her first visit in a preacher's home and she wasn't sure of the protocol.

She relaxed as they exchanged some stories of their recent past, their arrival in Brentville, and some of their first impressions.

It was midafternoon when Jill thanked them and said goodbye.

She decided to put on her walking shoes this time before tottering down the lane.

Straightening up, she started home. Even with Dan gone, this had been a good weekend. She wondered if the whole week would go as well as its beginning.

If Gordon and Mister Webber stay out of the picture, that would help.

Chapter 11

Jill sat at her desk Monday morning, reviewing the day's lessons, when she heard shouting outside.

Oh bother. This isn't a good start to the week.

She stepped outside in time to see Mike Orlick circling Randy Turner.

"Button your shirt, Randy," Mike taunted. "Girls like a guy to be neat—don't they, Melissa?"

Melissa stood nervously smoothing her skirt.

"Whatcha got to say, big guy?" Mike said.

Jill was about to intervene when Butch Taylor arrived.

"Pick on someone your own size, you bully," Butch growled.

"Hey, I'm not touching him," Mike argued. "Just having a little fun."

"It doesn't look like fun to me. Fun is only fun when everyone is laughing. Give it a break."

Butch came closer to the group and Mike turned and slunk toward the ball diamond.

Seeing Jill, he defended himself. "I wasn't going to hit him. I thought he was bothering Melissa."

Jill raised an eyebrow in surprise. "It looked like Melissa was more bothered by your taunts than by Randy's shirt button," she replied evenly. "Try to imagine how you would feel if you were Randy and someone as big as you was making trouble."

"See? No one ever takes my side." Mike kept walking toward the ball diamond.

Jill sighed. *This one is going to take patience. Something is bothering him besides Randy befriending Melissa. I wonder what gives him his mean streak? I wonder how I'm going to deal with it.*

It was time to ring the bell and start the week. Jill let Teresa stand on the step and swing the bell while Jill stood in the doorway to greet the students.

Marie paused, squinting up at Jill. "Mike is always picking fights," Marie offered. "Last year he—"

"This is a new year," Jill interrupted. "Let's not tattle about last year."

"I wasn't tattling." Marie looked offended. "I thought you should know."

Jill patted Marie on the shoulder. "I'll just let everyone have a fresh start. How's that? It's a new year for everyone. If I see Mike picking fights this year, I'll have to deal with it."

Marie straggled into the school and sat down.

Jill followed and had the class rise to sing *Oh Canada* and say the Lord's Prayer.

The morning passed quickly.

She helped Ivan Kolisnyk, who was struggling with English. Then she called Randy over.

"Randy, you know Ivan is new at the school. Would you mind reading this book to him and showing him the pictures? I think it would help him to improve his English faster."

Randy agreed happily. "If you want, Miss Jackson, I can read to him everyday."

"I think that would be great. I'll try to find enough books."

Randy is only nine, but he has a sensitive heart. I can trust him with Ivan. Now, how can I find the key to Mike?

Jill noticed Honey Wheeler walking up to the pencil sharpener. Honey managed to pat her hair and stop to pull up her socks in one short walk. Obviously, she liked to attract attention to herself and her stylish outfits.

"Honey, how many times do you need to sharpen your pencil?" Jill asked. "That's two times already this morning."

"I just like a sharp point," she replied, holding up the pencil like a dart so Jill could see it.

"She just likes for us to see her," Mike observed, looking over the book he was holding. "She's too stuck-up to be friends."

Honey sniffed and went back to her seat.

Mike's right on in that assessment.

At noon, the class all went outside to eat their lunches.

"Will you come out and skip today?" Teresa asked, pausing at her desk.

Jill smiled at Teresa. "I'm not sure, but thanks for asking. Now, don't forget to leave your glasses on your desk. You don't want to break them while you're having fun."

Jill poured a cup of coffee from her thermos and took out a sandwich. She eyed it before taking a bite. For a change from peanut butter and honey, she had tried a bottle of sandwich spread. Somehow it didn't appeal to her. She ate part of it, folded it back in the wax paper, and took out her apple and a fresh carrot while mulling over the students she was getting to know.

Her biggest concerns were Melissa Webber in Grade Three and Mike Orlick in Grade Seven. Melissa was doing well in her work and showed signs of artistic talent. What was it about this appealing little girl that puzzled her?

Mike Orlick was a different concern. Was his habit of provoking other students a cover-up? He was a poor reader. Did that make him feel inferior? Did he have a need to appear tough? She smiled, thinking of his droll assessment of Honey Wheeler.

Jill remembered Dan's warning: "You can only do so much."

True. She'd have to watch where to draw the line between getting to know the kids and getting too involved in their lives.

Jill checked the clock, stretched, and went to ring the bell.

"That was fun," Randy offered when he scooted back inside. "We had a great ballgame. Melissa got to first base."

Honey was next. She paused to straighten her skirt. "Sure makes me sweaty in the sun. I'll take a nice bubble-bath when I get home."

Bubble bath? What child in Grade Three thinks of a bubble bath and sweat when she's supposed to be having fun?

"Can I stay after school and help you clean the boards and stuff?" Sharon asked as she came into the classroom. "Mom said it would be okay to stay if you needed me."

"It would be great to have some help with clean-up, Sharon."

Jill smiled appreciatively and Sharon happily flipped a fraying braid over her shoulder as she found her seat.

I'm lucky to have such a nice bunch of students for my first school. There's challenges, but I can handle them. I just hope I can learn how to teach eight different grades at once. Well, others have done it, and so will I.

Jill stood up to start the afternoon with the class. "We'll take extra time today to read our favorite books," she said. "You can get them out now."

She watched as they pulled books from their desks.

"Larry, what book are you reading?"

"*Winnie the Pooh and Some Bees.*"

"Good choice. Are some of the words too hard for you?"

"Yup," Larry said. "But I just guess what fits the story and keep going. I like Winnie the Pooh."

"Good for you. Sharon, what are you reading?"

"I've got *The Lion, the Witch, and the Wardrobe*, the same book you're reading out loud to us. But I can go faster when I read to myself. So far the beavers, Mr. Tumnus, and Lucy are my favorite characters."

"Lucy was my favorite, too," Jill said with a smile. "Okay, let's be quiet and enjoy our books."

Jill savored the quiet and the time to just sit and watch the students. Mike slouched in his desk, pretending to read. Ivan used his finger to keep his place in the book he was reading. Honey patted her curls as she turned a page.

Jill let them read until recess.

After recess, while the students were working on their own, she heard a vehicle coming up the gravel road.

Oh no. Not Gordon again.

She glanced out the window and saw a car pull into the school grounds. The car door slammed shut and soon she heard footsteps clomping up to the door. She glanced up to see burly Steve Webber standing with his hat in his hand.

"Excuse me, miss, but I'm on my way home and thought I'd give Melissa a ride—save her from walking."

Jill glanced at Melissa. It was evident she was uneasy, but what could Jill do?

"Well, it's not a stormy day, but I guess I can dismiss her early. I would really appreciate a note, though, when you want a student before dismissal."

"Sure, miss. I didn't realize it was a federal case to pick up my own daughter twenty minutes early."

Mr. Webber's voice was definitely tinged with sarcasm and his face was reddening.

"Go ahead and get your things, Melissa," Jill said. "We'll see you in the morning."

"Could you hurry a little, Melissa?" her father said. "I don't have all afternoon to stand here."

Steve Webber already had his cap back on his head as Melissa hurried toward the door. As soon as it closed, the other students made comments which only added to Jill's misgivings.

"He's a bad one, miss," Butch said. "I used to deliver eggs there, but he gave me the creeps. I asked Mom to stop selling to him."

"Poor Melissa," added Randy. "I think she's scared of him."

"I don't know him yet," commented Jill. Changing the subject, she added, "It's so close to dismissal. Let's put away our books, tidy up, and get out a few minutes early."

Mike Orlick slammed his book shut. "Great!"

Soon they were all gone, except Sharon, who stayed behind to help clean the boards and brushes, and Butch, who got the broom to sweep the floor. Jill started working on her lesson plans.

Chapter 12

After locking the school, Jill strolled to her teacherage. Twilight was coming earlier. Most of the leaves had fallen from the trees and she could smell the smoke as someone in the area burned raked-up leaves. Jill scuffed her foot through some dry leaves along the path. She enjoyed the crackle as she put weight on them.

Too bad I don't have a whole pile to jump in! Guess I'm still a kid, just in an adult body.

She pushed open the door and considered what to have for supper. Maybe it was time for macaroni and cheese—and a can of tuna. She set the pot of water to boiling. There was still a little cake left, too.

Checking her phone list, she dialed Linda.

"Linda, how's it going?"

Linda chuckled. "Well, I should ask you the same question."

Jill laughed. "How about coming for tea after supper? It's my turn to pour."

"You're on. I'll come after I finish supper dishes. Thanks."

Jill had just opened the can of tuna when the phone rang. It was Dan.

"Hey, Jill. What's new in the life of the teacher?"

"Well, one thing is new. Melissa Webber's dad showed up at school."

"What did he want? Did he give you trouble?"

"No," she said. "He just wanted to take Melissa out of class early. He didn't take kindly to my request that in the future I'd appreciate a note if he wanted to take a student out of school before dismissal. Melissa looked anxious, but I had to let her go. I know one thing: I wouldn't want to antagonize the guy."

"Don't think about him. He's just throwing his weight around. I've got a good alternative for when he pops into your mind."

"What's that?"

Dan laughed. "Just think about me instead."

Jill joined in the laughter. "One thing is sure. It's a much more pleasant alternative."

"Actually, I'm calling to see what you're doing tomorrow after school," Dan said. "I'd like to pick you up for supper. Wear slacks and we could go roller-skating afterwards. They'll soon close the rink for the winter."

"Oh, that sounds great. What time do you want me to be ready?"

"Well, I should be off work by five o'clock, so I could be at your place by five-thirty."

"I'm ready for a break. It will be good to see you."

Jill hung up, a little short of breath. Talking to Dan did that to her.

She ate her macaroni and tuna, thinking about how nice it would be to have a real supper—and Dan as her companion.

Linda arrived and they sat at the kitchen table sipping tea, nibbling some cake, and visiting.

"I'm so glad to find a friend close by," Linda confided.

"Well, I'm in the same boat. You're a gift."

They soon felt like they had been friends for a long time.

Jill decided she could get some advice on what to do about Gordon Curtiss. She recounted the class interruption, the Saturday shopping episode, and Gordon parking to check on her Saturday afternoon.

"I don't like the sound of it, Jill," Linda said. "For goodness sake, don't go out with him. That would just encourage him to keep pestering you."

"I can't imagine ever going out willingly with Gordon. I've started dating a fellow who has Gordon beat by a country mile." Jill smiled just thinking about Dan.

"Seems like he's pretty special, judging by the look in your eye." Linda looked pensively at Jill. "One of these days, I need to tell you something of my story. But I'll save it for another time. It'll get dark soon and I should be getting home."

Linda carried her cup to the sink.

"Thanks for asking me over," Linda said. "I'll look forward to seeing you again soon."

Linda opened the door, turned, and waved. Soon, she was briskly walking up the path.

Jill locked the door and pulled the blinds.

I wonder what she's going to tell me? And when? Not to mention, where will Dan take me for supper tomorrow? What slacks should I wear? I've really only got one pair that are decent, so they'll have to do.

She would be short of planning time tomorrow after school, so Jill sat down and made some notes for Wednesday. Somehow, the thought of going back to the school this late in the evening made her a little uneasy.

Before she got ready for bed, she called home.

Mom answered. She was glad to hear about Jill's new friend, and also glad that the cake had lasted until Linda came.

"How's Dad?" Jill asked.

"Oh, he's doing okay. And Joanne got a promotion at work." Mom added that part with a touch of pride in her voice.

"I'm glad Dad is feeling okay. Give Joanne my congrats. I'd better sign off. Tomorrow is a new day."

Jill hung up feeling just a little sour. *Why does Joanne always have to figure in the conversation? Well, it's been a good day. Tomorrow will be great. I'm not going to let a Joanne report spoil things.*

Jill had a leisurely soak in the tub, then climbed into bed thinking of supper, roller-skating, and Dan.

Chapter 13

Jill closed her plan book early on Tuesday afternoon.

That will have to do for tomorrow. Tonight I've got something more important.

She hurried up the walk, barely glancing at the bush which had lost most of the red leaves she had enjoyed so much. Once inside, she turned on the tub taps. While the water filled, she laid out her outfit.

I'm glad my good slacks are black. That should help hide my hips. Should I wear the blue top or the red? Guess I'll take the red and wear my black cardigan in case it gets cool.

She would take a quick dunk in the tub. Jill glanced at the time. There was still an hour before Dan arrived. She could slow down—everything but her heart, which insisted on racing as she thought of the coming evening.

Eyebrows plucked, cowlick settled properly, dressed carefully, Jill sat in her easy chair and tried to read while she waited.

Finally she heard Dan's truck. She watched him saunter to her door, then stood up to welcome him.

"Wow," he said. "Don't you look good?"

Jill relished the compliment and searched for one to give in return.

Instead she just said, "Thanks. I want to look good when I go out with you. You always look so… so…" Dan's eyebrow lifted, waiting. "You always look so dashing," she finished a little lamely.

Dan enjoyed her fluster as much as the compliment.

"Enough talking," he said. "We need to be eating."

He helped her into her sweater and then into his pickup truck.

Dan slid in and started the engine. "Someday I'll get a car," he said, "but for now I really need this baby."

"What a splendid evening to be going someplace," Jill observed contentedly.

She glanced at Linda's place as they drove by. Sure enough, Linda was in her garden. It looked like Sharon was with her.

Dusk was deepening. It was a cozy feeling to be in the darkening cab with Dan.

"How's this?" Dan glanced at her as they pulled into the restaurant parking lot.

"This looks super. I've never eaten here before."

I might as well admit I've hardly eaten in any restaurant—especially one that looks this nice.

Dan found a quiet booth beside a window. The waiter lit the candle on the table and Jill picked up her menu.

"What do you recommend?" Jill waited, hoping for Dan to suggest something that would give her an idea of how much he wanted to spend. Waiting for her first paycheck, she was very conscious of expenses.

"You'd be surprised, but I happen to like liver and onions."

Jill tried not to look a little ill.

"How about the breaded veal cutlets? I'll bet you'd like that," Dan added. "They have a good chef here, so you can't go wrong."

Jill returned her attention to the menu. "I think the breaded veal cutlets do sound good. That's what I'll take. If they have baked potatoes, I'd really like that."

"Consider it done. If the lady wants a baked potato, she'll have one."

Pencil poised, the waiter came over. His white shirt sleeves were rolled up and he wore black trousers with a black vest.

"What would the lady like tonight?"

He directed the question to Dan, who answered easily. "We'll each have a dinner salad with your house dressing. The lady wants the veal cutlets with a baked potato, and I'll have the liver—no onions."

Jill wasn't sure, but she thought he winked when requesting no onions.

"Tea or coffee?" Dan asked Jill.

"Tea, please," she replied and then sat back to enjoy the coming meal.

The restaurant wasn't crowded, so occasionally she heard music in the background. The current tune was "River of No Return."

"Tell me about the reunion," she began. "You said your folks enjoyed the trip. Did you have lots of relatives there? Do you have these reunions regularly?"

"Whoa." Dan chuckled. "One question at a time. The reunion was good. There were cousins I'd never met—and likely won't see again unless we have another reunion. They live in Ontario. Mom and Dad really enjoyed the reunion although travelling isn't high on their list of fun things to do. This was the first reunion in about twenty years, so maybe you could say we 'regularly' have a reunion every two decades." Suddenly, he changed the subject. "How about your family? Do you have reunions and get-togethers? I don't even know how many are in your family. I just consider myself lucky that we both knew Joe Conroy and he introduced us."

"I'm glad, too." She smiled. "Anyway, I have a younger sister, Joanne. She works at Eatons in ladies fashions. We don't seem to have a lot in common. Her main interest is having an expensive wardrobe. I wanted to go to school and then teach. Dad is a dear. He has a great sense of humor and runs a garage. Mom is a fuss budget… always concerned about what people think, and getting the news while she has her hair done every week. I know she cares about us both, but Joanne is her favorite. Dad treats us each the same."

The waiter arrived with their salads and placed them carefully on the table. Jill was glad of the interruption.

Why do thoughts of Joanne seem to bother me? Anyway, I won't let her mess up this perfect evening.

"More hot water for your tea, miss?" The waiter was back.

"Thanks. That would be lovely."

"Coffee, sir?" The waiter held the carafe and Dan nodded.

Dinner passed leisurely. The street lights of Saskatoon were starting to shine.

"Should be a perfect evening for roller-skating," Dan said as they finished up. "Are you ready? I'm not a good skater, but I'll try not to pull you down on the rink."

Dan paid the bill and they left the restaurant.

The Eighth Street roller rink wasn't a long drive from the restaurant, so they could already hear the music before they arrived. Jill's toes were tapping.

Dan helped her put the skates on over her saddle oxfords and tightened the key.

"That okay, or do you want it tighter?"

"I'm not a skating pro, but it feels fine. Let's try."

Dan took her arm and they stepped onto the rink. They were soon gliding in step to the music.

"You know what?" Dan asked, looking sideways at Jill. "I think I skate better when I'm hanging onto you!"

Jill laughed. "Well, I know for sure I skate better when I have support. For people who don't skate often, I'd say we're doing pretty well."

Just then, a skater cut in front of them and they nearly lost their balance, bumping into the wooden fence around the rink.

Jill rubbed her elbow. "Spoke too soon, I guess."

After a few more rounds, they turned in their skates and headed to the pickup.

"That was sure fun," Jill commented. "Thanks for such a nice evening."

Dan helped her into the truck and they started back to Brentville.

"If you slid a little closer this way, I could practice driving with one arm," Dan said.

Jill knew she was blushing as she slid across the seat and snuggled close to Dan. It only took a moment before his arm was around her shoulder. She sighed contentedly.

"Comfortable?" he asked.

"Oh, yes."

Jill laid her head on Dan's shoulder.

All too soon, they were back at the teacherage. Dan turned toward her, kissed her slowly, and then walked her to the door.

"Just one more," he said and kissed her again before she went inside. "Don't forget to lock the door."

With that, he turned and was gone.

Chapter 14

∿

Today's payday. At last! I'll try my budget and hope it works. Dinner with Mom and Dad is my top priority…

Jill was at the school steps and ready to face the day.

"Good morning, Ivan." She bent down to look the young boy in the eye.

"How do you do?" Ivan said, practicing his formal English. "I am fine."

"Good work, Ivan." Jill rubbed his brush cut lightly. "Keep it up. You're learning your English quite quickly."

Ivan beamed.

"Larry, what did you do last evening?" she asked next.

"Helped feed the cows and pigs and then went riding on my horse," Larry answered.

"My goodness, I didn't know you helped on the farm that much. Good for you. Let me feel your muscles."

Larry proudly flexed his arm for her.

"Do you have running water at the farm, or do you have to haul it in for the animals?" Jill asked.

"Oh, we have a well. It runs all year. We get all our water from the well, even for the house."

"That's a lot of work, isn't it? But then, at least you have it on the yard."

"That's what Dad says. But Mom would like a pipe to the house."

"It would be handy for her, I'm sure."

That answers my question about Larry's grubby looks. Poor kid. No running water in this day and age. No wonder he has BO. But he's such a happy boy. I hope no one starts to tease him.

"I forgot to ask you the name of your horse," Jill said. "What do you call her?"

"It's a 'he' and I call him Trigger. Like Roy Rogers' horse." Larry shrugged his shoulders and grinned.

It was time to ring the bell.

Marie Stollery came up to them, squinting at Jill. "Miss Jackson?"

"Is this a tattletale, Marie?"

Marie continued squinting at Jill. "No. I just thought I should tell you what Mike said to Randy."

"Do you think Randy was offended, or do you just want to get Mike into trouble?" Jill asked, peering at Marie.

I need to help her know what is tattling. And I wonder if she needs glasses? She squints so much.

Marie looked a little puzzled. "I'm not sure, so I guess I'll just go in."

Jill patted Marie on the shoulder. "That's probably a good idea for now. Sometimes it is hard to know the difference between tattling to get someone into trouble and reporting something that needs attention."

By recess, Jill was ready for a cup of coffee from her thermos. At noon, she was beginning to feel hungry for a sandwich. By evening, she was clutching her first paycheck.

The folks will be here soon to pick me up and take me to the bank. Then I'll take them to dinner. First time. And about time.

Jill settled at her desk to do some brief lesson plans but paused when she heard a step at the door.

"Good night, Miss Jackson."

Jill looked up to see Melissa standing tentatively in the school doorway.

"Oh, Melissa. I didn't know you were still here." Jill smiled. "Do you want to come in and visit a few minutes?"

Melissa paused briefly. "I'd better get home. I've been sitting in the sun, thinking, and now I'm late. Bye."

She turned and was gone.

Jill sighed. Melissa was such a sweet child. What was it that concerned her? What was that look in Melissa's eyes that she couldn't fathom?

Little did Jill guess that the answer would unfold that very evening, but she wouldn't know or understand it until many weeks later.

Chapter 15

Melissa woke with a lump in her stomach. Was she dreaming or had she heard a step in the hall? Yes, there it was—the creak in the hall floor. She turned over carefully to face the wall, pulling her knees up tightly to her chest. Maybe if she could pretend she was asleep…

"Roll over, you little sweetheart. Don't play hard to get with me," she heard her father whisper. "When you smiled at me at supper, I knew you wanted me to come."

Smiled at him? Melissa couldn't recall smiling. She had to be careful not to do that again. Reluctantly, she rolled over to face her father. He was looking down at her with that look she feared and hated.

"Time to play Snow Angel, isn't it? Remember to spread your arm-wings so you can fold them over me. And don't forget to spread your legs out over the snow sheets."

Melissa shuddered. She knew better than to cry or beg. That made him angry and rough. She wondered where her mother was. Was her mother asleep when he slipped out of bed? Why didn't she wake up and come to help her?

Melissa sighed as she made herself into the pretend snow angel on the bed. Her father seemed to think pretending snow angel made this a fun game. She cringed as she prepared for the pain. Why did her father want to hurt her? Did other fathers do this to their daughters?

As her father leaned over her, she tried to turn her face.

He's been eating onions again, she thought as her father pulled her face toward his.

Finally, it was over.

"You're the best girl," he said as he pulled up his pajamas and patted her head. Then he left her room.

Now she could cry. He was gone.

Chapter 16

Monday morning, when Jill arrived at the school, Melissa was already there, sitting alone on a swing. She looked so downcast.

Jill walked over to her. "Good morning, Melissa."

Melissa answered, but without looking up at Jill. "Morning."

"Is something wrong? Can I help?"

"No thanks. I'm okay."

It was obvious that Melissa didn't want to talk about whatever was bothering her.

"If I can help, let me know."

Jill turned and walked a little reluctantly to the school. All she could do was watch for opportunities to let Melissa know that she was special. And she could pray.

"Hey, Melissa. Come and play catch."

Melissa turned to see Randy lofting a ball from one hand to the other. Randy—uncoordinated Randy—was such a thoughtful child.

"No thanks, Randy. I'd just like to sit awhile."

"See, Randy," Mike taunted. "The princess doesn't want to get her hands dirty playing ball."

"Not true, Randy. Can't I just sit awhile without you butting in?"

Jill could hardly believe her ears. Melissa was actually defending herself. But Mike was strolling to the ball diamond as Butch approached. Apparently Melissa wasn't going to have much time to sit quietly alone!

It was time to ring the bell.

The students filed in, Melissa entering last. Jill gave her a quick hug and a smile.

It was an uneventful morning. Mike produced a few titters as he mispronounced words while reading aloud. Jill was quick to squelch them, pointing out that everyone had areas where they did well and areas where they did not.

As she feared, Mike had to express his bravado. Teresa was the unlucky recipient. After his embarrassing reading, Mike lumbered up to the wastebasket with a paper to throw away. On the way up the aisle, he managed to stumble and shove the books off Teresa's desk.

"Oh, I'm so sorry, my lady." Mike did an exaggerated bow, pretending to doff a hat. "Too bad your books were hanging over the edge."

Teresa pushed her glasses higher and glared at Mike. "You know good and well that you did that on purpose."

"I told you I'm sorry," Mike said, trying to look offended.

"Well, if you're so sorry, you can pick them up," Teresa challenged.

At this point, Jill joined in. "She's right, Mike. Show you're sorry by picking up the books."

Everyone was watching now. Jill could tell he was weighing his options.

What will I do if he refuses? He's sure too big for me to strap.

She gave a deep sigh of relief when Mike picked up the books, bowed to Teresa, and put them on the middle of her desk.

"You could say 'thank you,' Teresa."

Teresa's half-hearted thanks ended that situation. There were no more challenges that morning.

In the afternoon, Jill announced plans for Thanksgiving. They talked about the first Thanksgiving and the gratitude of the Pilgrims for surviving and for having a harvest. They planned some classroom decorations. Jill introduced "Father, We Thank Thee," and they began learning a hymn of thanks.

"How would it be if we have a program the last hour on Friday before Thanksgiving?" Jill asked. "You can invite your folks or your grandparents to come at ten minutes to three on October 7. I know some of them will be at work, but if they come they can see our decorations, look at your work, and hear you sing your Thanksgiving hymn."

I'll also get to meet some other parents, I hope, and the kids will have an incentive to do their best.

"I'll ask Mom if she would make some cookies," Sharon offered.

Mike laughed. "If she's a good cook, tell her to bring lots."

"Would you want us to dress up for the program?" Honey asked.

"Just wear your usual school clothes," Jill said. "We'll dress up more for our Christmas program."

How could a child in Grade Three be so clothing conscious?

Melissa raised her hand.

"Yes, Melissa?"

She stood, smoothing her skirt. "If I could have some extra paper, could I stay in some noon hours and draw a special picture? I mean, if you have one I could sort of copy, I'd try." She sat down.

"That would be wonderful, Melissa. I know you have a special talent in art. I would be happy to give you extra paper."

Jill was thrilled at Melissa's participation, and Melissa looked happy to have her offer accepted.

"I'm not a good singer, Miss Jackson," Butch added, "but I'd enjoy trying."

"Great. I'm excited about our celebration. And one more thing. I'm thankful to be your teacher. You're a great bunch of students. Now, let's clean up under our desks and get ready to go home."

Sharon raised her hand. "Can I clean the brushes again, Miss Jackson?"

"I'd be happy for you to do that, Sharon. Just don't clap them too near your face and get chalk dust on yourself."

Jill sat at her desk to plan tomorrow's lessons, but her thoughts quickly strayed.

Thanksgiving weekend. A long weekend with holiday Monday. What will I do with it? I think I'll call Marg West. Marg and I spent so much time together at Teacher's College, and now it seems like ages since we saw each other. She'll be ready for a weekend in Saskatoon. Marg could stay with me… we'll talk and nibble! Maybe Dan's friend Joe would even double-date. Hey, that's beginning to sound like fun. I'll make some phone calls.

"Is that everything, Miss Jackson?" Sharon was standing at her desk.

"Yes, I think so. Thanks so much for helping."

Jill picked up her books and headed to the door with Sharon. First she'd start planning the Thanksgiving long weekend, then she'd plan her lessons for tomorrow.

Chapter 17

"Now, where's Marg's phone number?" Jill muttered to herself while searching for her phone book. "I hope she's home."

Jill dialed quickly, flipping over the egg timer when Marg answered. The egg timer took exactly three minutes for the sand to sift through the tiny hourglass shape, which is why Jill used it for long distance calls. After three minutes on the phone, the rates went up and she couldn't afford much extra time.

"Marg, how are you doing?"

"Jill! What a surprise. What's up?"

"Why don't you leave right after school the Friday before Thanksgiving, and come to stay here? We'll have a ball visiting. And I'll ask Dan if he has a buddy so we can double-date."

"Who's Dan?"

"I'll tell you all about it when you get here. Takes too much time on long distance, but please say you'll come. I can't wait to see you and gab. Oh, please come. I'll write to you and tell you how to get here."

"You know what?"

Jill held her breath.

"It sounds great and I'd love to come," Marg finished.

"Wonderful, wonderful. I'll start planning. It was just a brainwave this afternoon when we were talking about Thanksgiving. Oops—our three minutes are almost up. I'll write tonight."

"See you for Thanksgiving weekend. Bye for now."

Jill hung up and danced around the kitchen. Then she grabbed a pen and paper. "I'd better plan some menus," she announced to the table as she pulled up a chair.

Where did I put my cookbook? She bounced up to look in her bookshelf. It held mostly papers and a stack of magazines, but under one pile she found the cookbook and triumphantly pulled it out.

Just as she started looking for a meatloaf recipe, the phone rang.

"How's it going, Teach?"

"Oh, Dan, I've got great news. Did I mention my friend, Marg West? We went to Teacher's College together and she's teaching just north of Saskatoon. Anyway, she's lots of fun, and she's going to come here for Thanksgiving weekend. Do you think Joe would double-date with us? Marg is fun—and she's good looking. I think Joe would like her—at least for a weekend."

"Whoa. Maybe I already have some plans for that weekend."

"Oh, Dan, I'm sorry. I should have asked. I just thought of all this at school when we were talking about Thanksgiving plans. I was so excited that I rushed home to phone Marg." Jill's heart sank. "It seemed like such a good idea, I didn't think to ask you first."

Dan chuckled. "I'll let you off this time. Your idea just improves mine."

"What's that?"

"I was going to wrangle an invitation for dinner at your place one evening. Then I thought we might have a game of Monopoly. If the weather is good, we could have a wienie roast at Jill's Cookhouse. There's a winding walk along the riverbank and we could go to the dam and sit and watch awhile—maybe walk across the train trestle. Or we could even pack a lunch and drive to Pike Lake… maybe rent a boat."

"Oh, Dan. That sounds super."

"And Joe is free as a breeze, so I'm sure he would join us and squire your friend. But I'll ask before I make plans for him."

Jill got the hint and smiled. "Good idea. Some folks just rush in and make plans without asking—not mentioning any names."

"Don't scold yourself. Save that for the kids. And, by the way, are they behaving?"

"Just great. I'm lucky to start with such good kids. Melissa still troubles me. She arrived this morning looking so downhearted. Just sat by herself on a swing."

"Don't forget my warning," Dan said. "You can't fix everything for everyone. Just do what you can."

"I can't do anything for Melissa because I don't know if—or what—her problem is. Somehow I think it has something to do with her dad. She didn't look too happy when he picked her up early this week."

"Well, don't dwell on it. If there's something you should do, you'll know when the time comes. Now, let's plan that weekend."

"You bet. Oh, Dan, I'm so excited just thinking about it."

Dan chuckled. "I can hear you smiling over the phone."

"For the Friday night dinner invitation you were thinking about, if we have it a little later, Marg can get here. I thought if I mixed a meatloaf on Thursday night, it would be ready for the oven after school. Then we'll have baked potatoes and a salad…"

"I'm hungry already. How would it be if I pick up some ice cream and chocolate sauce for dessert?"

Jill sighed. "That sounds great. Then I won't have to worry about dessert. On Saturday, we could meet here for bacon and eggs, or Marg could bring me in and we could go to a restaurant. We'll pack a lunch and drive to Pike Lake—or go for the hike and down to the dam. The weekend will be over before we know it. Oh, it's going to be so much fun."

"How about this weekend? Do you feel like bowling Friday night? You might want to practice a little before the four of us start keeping score."

Dan chuckled, but Jill was forced to admit, "If I break one hundred at bowling, I'll consider it a good game."

"Hey, the point is to have fun. I can even laugh when I throw a gutter ball."

"That's good news. And for the answer to your question, I'd love to practice this Friday. I might surprise us both and get a strike or two!"

"Time to make supper here. The folks are out and I'm stuck making supper for myself." Dan imitated a groan.

"That's tough," Jill mocked. "Now you have an idea what it's like to make supper every night for one person to eat… that is, except when a friend takes you to a nice restaurant. Anyway, talk to you soon. Have a good evening. And I hope Joe agrees to our weekend."

"I'll let you know," Dan advised before hanging up.

Jill reached for a slice of brown bread along with the peanut butter and honey.

This still tastes pretty good with some garden carrots and a glass of milk.

Chapter 18

Time flew until Thanksgiving weekend. Melissa's picture of the Pilgrims and Indians enjoying the first Thanksgiving dinner together was given a prominent place of display. The entire class helped make a mural, each child choosing some aspect of Thanksgiving to draw and include. Everyone learned the tune and two verses of "Father, We Thank Thee." Jill had the children print and decorate invitations to take home to their parents. She hoped some would come for the short program.

During all the flurry, Jill prepared lessons and planned for her upcoming Thanksgiving weekend with Marg. It seemed she was energized by all the activity and deadlines.

Friday afternoon before the parents came, Linda arrived with cookies for everyone.

"Oh, Linda, I'm so glad you could come," Jill said. "I really don't know how many parents will make it for the afternoon, but the kids have worked hard and I hope some parents can come."

"Jill, it's a great idea to let them come and see their kids in the classroom. I talked to a couple of mothers who will be here."

"Whoever comes, comes. Thanks for bringing the cookies. That is special for the kids. You're so thoughtful."

"There have been times when I didn't think, and I lived to regret it," Linda said soberly as she turned to set out the cookies.

I wonder what she means by that. Maybe it's what she wants to talk about someday. Well, the timing will be hers. I won't ask questions.

Right after recess, some parents arrived. Marcie Webber walked up the road. She looked nervous in her homemade dress, but she was very pleasant as she greeted Jill. She then looked for Melissa and went to talk to her.

Jill was surprised and pleased when Helen Gilmore arrived.

"It's great you could join us," Jill told the pastor's wife. "Thanks for coming. I know some of these kids come to church, so they'll be glad you came. Especially if their folks can't make it, they'll look to you to be their visitor."

Ann Wheeler arrived wearing a lovely dress and high heels. She had just had her hair done. Jill felt dowdy by comparison, but was glad to welcome Ann.

"Mrs. Wheeler, I'm so glad you could come. I think this is the first time we've actually met. You can visit Honey at her desk and she'll show you some of her work."

Mrs. Wheeler nodded. "I can't stay too long. The dog needs to get to the groomer today. My husband fusses over Prince. He's a purebred poodle and Ken wants him groomed regularly."

Mrs. Wheeler walked over to Honey's desk, smoothed her hair, and checked her daughter's work carefully.

That's four so far—and we have another ten minutes before we start. It's so interesting to be able to talk to the parents and see them with their kids.

Tina Turner arrived. She had a slight limp. Randy had mentioned that his mom had had polio a few years earlier.

Jill was also pleased to see Andy Taylor. "I know you're busy at the farm," she said. "Thanks so much for taking time to come."

Andy twisted the cap in his hands. "Well, I'm both mother and father to Butch, so I like to show up when I can."

"You're doing a good job. Butch is a fine, stable young man."

Andy mumbled his thanks, but Jill knew he was encouraged by her comments.

"Hello," Jill said, turning to greet another arriving mother. "Welcome. I'm Jill Jackson."

Whose mom is this?

She was relieved as she glanced at the class and saw Ivan Kolisnyk beckoning and smiling.

"You must be Mrs. Kolisnyk." Jill smiled and gestured toward Ivan. "He would like to show you his work."

Mrs. Kolisnyk started tentatively toward Ivan's desk.

How much English does she understand? What a brave woman to come to the school when she has such a limited vocabulary.

Jill glanced at the clock: it was time to begin their short program. She glanced out the window at the road and saw the dust rolling. They would wait a few minutes for the latecomer.

She gasped when she realized the vehicle belonged to Gordon Curtiss.

Jill groaned and made a beeline for Linda. "Linda, that vehicle burning up the road is the guy who bugged me when we were shopping. Please, can you go out on the step and turn him away before he comes in? Tell him this is a Thanksgiving program for parents only. Oh, Linda, what will I do if he insists on coming in?"

"Consider it done. He won't come in." Linda's face was set and she marched to the door while Jill somewhat shakily made her way to the front.

"This is the Thanksgiving weekend," she began. "Monday is a school holiday and I hope you all have a good family time together."

Jill glanced at the parents. Some had managed to sit in the desks beside their children while others were grouped at the back.

Too bad we don't have a few chairs here for something like this. I should get some before we do this again.

"We would like to sing a Thanksgiving song for you," Jill said. "It was written many years ago. Class, would you come up front now?"

Jill gave them the pitch and they started in. She could hear Helen Gilmore's strong soprano giving the children support as they sang:

"Father, we thank Thee for the night
And for the pleasant morning light
For rest and food and loving care
And all that makes the day so fair.
"Help us to do the things we should
To be to others kind and good
In all our work and all our play
To love Thee better everyday."

The parents clapped, and then the children returned to their seats. Meanwhile, Jill was relieved to see Linda come back into the school as Gordon's truck made a quick exit.

A friend in need is a friend, indeed. What a close call. What an embarrassment it would have been if he had managed to come in. Thank goodness for Linda!

She continued more confidently. "Sharon Martins wrote a Thanksgiving poem and we'd like her to come up and read it for you."

Sharon rubbed her eye, flipped a braid behind her shoulder, and began. Jill smiled. For a student in Grade Five, it was a good poem.

When she finished, everyone clapped and Sharon sat down.

"Now, we just want you to look at the artwork the children have done. Everyone worked on the mural and Melissa Webber drew this one special picture."

Jill noticed Marcie Webber's look of surprise and pleasure.

"Linda Martins brought cookies, and there is some juice at the back," Jill told them. "Enjoy yourselves. We are so glad you came."

Ann Wheeler excused herself. "I need to get to the groomers," she confided. "Could Honey leave with me now?"

"Of course. School is over for the day. Have a good weekend."

Jill waved at Honey as she left with her mother.

Other parents stayed, chatted, and made comments about their children's work. Everyone enjoyed the cookies and juice.

At ten minutes to four, Jill asked the children to pick up around their desks and get ready for dismissal.

"Thanks to each of you parents who took time to come. And thanks to Helen Gilmore for joining us. Thanks to Linda Martins for the cookies. Class, you did a good job singing and doing the artwork. I wish each of you a happy Thanksgiving weekend."

Jill felt happy and relieved as she saw everyone to the door.

"Butch, never mind sweeping up today," Jill said softly to him. "You can leave with your father."

Butch smiled and stepped up beside his dad.

Butch is almost the same height as his dad. It's nice to see they have such a good relationship. I wonder how Mrs. Taylor died—and how long ago.

After everyone was gone, Jill left the schoolhouse and locked the door. Looking at her watch, she hurried home.

Now to the big part of the weekend. I've looked forward to it so much, I hope I'm not disappointed. But I won't be. It will be wonderful.

She went in to check on supper plans.

Chapter 19

Jill turned on the oven, took the meatloaf from the fridge, and started scrubbing potatoes to get them ready to bake. "Now to set the table. Where is that tablecloth?" she said out loud to keep her thoughts straight. "Here we go." She flipped the tablecloth open with a flourish. "Now the plates and cutlery. Napkin under the fork, knife edge toward the plate… I'm glad Mom drilled all this into me."

The oven beeped when the temperature was hot enough, so she put the meatloaf in.

I'll give it a head start, then put in the potatoes. Sure don't want anyone getting sick on meat that isn't cooked long enough.

She glanced around. "Glasses. I need glasses for our drinks. And I'll get the coffee pot ready."

Things were going pretty well.

The phone rang and she hurried to answer.

"Hello." She could hear her own concern as she answered. *I hope that's not Marg saying she has car trouble and will be late.*

"Well, if it isn't Miss Priss."

Her heart sank as she recognized Gordon Curtiss on the line.

"Wouldn't let me into the school this afternoon, eh?"

"Gordon, the kids were performing a Thanksgiving program for their parents. It wasn't time for me to stop and visit."

What in the world can I say to get him off the line and still try to be polite?

"Well, if you want to visit, I can come out this evening," Gordon said.

Good grief. This is getting worse by the minute. He says he hates lying so I'll just tell him the truth.

"Gordon, I'm sorry, but this isn't a good time. A girlfriend is coming for the weekend, and my boyfriend is coming for supper. I know he wouldn't appreciate an extra guy for supper."

"A boyfriend? Why didn't you tell me before I made a fool of myself?"

"It's a recent development. I hope you can find a girlfriend, but right now it can't be me. I truly wish you well, but…"

The receiver slammed in her ear.

I fervently hope that slammed receiver is his farewell. So far, all he's done is make trouble for me. He's a mixed-up guy. I feel sorry for him. Looks like, where I'm concerned, he doesn't like lying. He doesn't like the truth, either! I wonder what happened to Wilma? Well, Wilma and I seem to be on two different paths now. I'll likely never know what happened.

Jill went into her bathroom to lay out towels for Marg, then added the potatoes to the oven rack, checked the clock, and sat down to wait for company.

It was only five-thirty when she heard Dan's truck pull in. Dan and Joe each jumped out and came to the door.

Jill opened it before they even knocked.

"I'm so glad you're here." She looked at Dan, and then Joe. Dan put the ice cream into the fridge freezer.

"Tell me about this Marg girl," Joe said.

"I'll let you make up your own mind—no preconceived notions," Jill said. "But I think you'll be able to stand her for a weekend. Personally, I think she's a lot of fun."

"That all the info I'll get?"

"She should be here in an hour, then you can make up your own mind. I'm so glad you agreed to double up for the weekend, so I hope you like her company."

"We'll see. I've never dated anyone I haven't met, so I'm a little leery."

"Well, thanks for taking the chance on her."

Jill glanced at Dan. He gave her a wink.

Does that mean Joe is pulling my leg about worrying, or does it mean Dan had to work to convince him to come?

"Hey, I'll bet that's Marg coming up the road," Jill said as she heard a car on the gravel outside.

Jill watched as Marg zoomed into the yard and parked.

"I think she's got a little lead in those feet. She really made good time." Jill laughed and went to the door.

Marg arrived talking. "Hmmm, that meatloaf smells good. I hope you guys aren't too hungry. I might eat it all. You can't tell how I've looked forward to getting out of the classroom cage this weekend."

Jill introduced Marg to Dan and Joe.

"Looks like we're sort of stuck with each other this weekend, Joe," Marg said. "But if you're Dan's friend, I'm sure you're a nice guy and it will be a great weekend."

"I didn't know you've met Dan," Joe puzzled.

"I did just now. And I trust Jill's taste. If you're Dan's friend, you're okay."

Joe chuckled and looked at Jill. "You know what? I think you're right. It will be a great weekend."

Jill privately heaved a sigh of relief.

"Want to wash up?" she asked Marg. "I think everything is nearly ready."

Marg headed to the bathroom while Jill went to the fridge to take out the salad, dressing, and sour cream for the potatoes. Dan and Joe followed her to the kitchen.

"Do you mind taking out the meatloaf, Dan?" she asked. "And please, put the potatoes in this bowl."

Marg joined them. "Anything I can do?"

"Sure," Jill said. "Take the drink orders. Water, milk, or ginger ale."

"Consider it done."

They all sat down. "Let's hold hands for grace. This is a special dinner." Jill reached for Dan's hand and Marg's, then thanked the Lord for Marg's safe trip, for the time together, and for the food.

"Now dig in," she announced happily.

Dan reached for the meatloaf and then passed it first to Jill.

Joe passed Marg the bowl of potatoes.

It's off to a good start, anyway. Let's hope it ends this well or better.

Chapter 20

"Great meatloaf," Joe said with a grin. "I couldn't have done better myself."

"A bachelor who cooks?" Jill asked.

"You bet. Macaroni and cheese, macaroni and bacon, macaroni and butter, and dessert can be macaroni and sugar." Joe laughed. "See why this meatloaf tastes so good?"

"Well, I've seen you dish up ice cream and put on sauce for a sundae," Dan offered. "Doesn't that count as cooking?"

They bantered back and forth throughout the meal.

"Time for the piece de resistance… or however you pronounce it. I made the dessert. Let me serve." With a flourish, Dan was at the freezer getting out the ice cream and dishing it up. "Any maraschino cherries for decoration?"

"Sorry," Jill said. "No go. It'll be good as is. Thanks for bringing it. I didn't have time to make a cake."

"Oh, just a minute," Marg said. "I need to check my suitcase." In a moment, Marg returned triumphantly carrying a small bag. "This is my hostess gift."

Opening the bag, she produced chocolate chip cookies.

"I'm impressed," Joe said, taking a bite.

When supper was over, they all cleared the table and set up Monopoly.

Dan grinned at Jill. "I like a game that takes a while. That way we can stay late."

Soon they were buying properties, houses, and then hotels. Joe had Park Place and Jill had Boardwalk. It took some wheeling and dealing, but Jill finally got Park Place and promptly put on hotels.

"Great place here to rest. Be sure to take a stop at either of these fine properties," Jill coaxed. But the dice let everyone pass for several rounds before Dan landed on Boardwalk. "Oh, good. My first customer."

Dan paid cheerfully, stroking her palm slightly with every bill he gave.

After a while, Jill offered to make hot chocolate.

"Great idea," Joe said. "Any popcorn to go with it?"

"That I have. Who wants to shake the pot of corn till it pops? I'll melt some butter."

"Since I asked for popcorn, I'd better get it popped. Besides, I haven't done anything yet for this supper." Joe got up, poured some kernels in the pot, and started shaking. Jill got the butter ready while Marg made hot chocolate.

Suddenly, Joe started yelping. Popcorn was starting to pop and fly over the edge of the pan. Jill grabbed the lid and Dan picked up stray popcorn.

"This isn't macaroni, you know," Jill told him. "You've got to extend your culinary skills if you're going to pop corn."

"Gotcha. Here's a bowl for starters. I'll do better on the next batch—I hope."

They settled in the living room with hot chocolate and popcorn.

After nearly an hour more of the game, Joe suggested, "Let's call it a draw. I'd like to just sit and visit awhile. Marg, tell us about life in the cage, as you put it."

Marg regaled them with some of her students' antics. Jill told them that she enjoyed teaching but was concerned about the occasional withdrawal of Melissa, one of her students.

"I warned that you can only do so much," Dan admonished.

"Yes, but she does worry me some."

"Let it go… at least for the weekend."

"Okay. I shouldn't have mentioned it."

It was soon time for Dan and Joe to leave.

"Great evening, Jill and Marg. Thanks for having us." Joe started for the door with Dan.

Dan paused. "How about meeting us in town for breakfast around nine? We'll buy, won't we, Joe?"

"Sure thing. Name the place and this bachelor will be there for real bacon and eggs."

Once the place was set, Dan and Joe got in Dan's truck and drove off.

Jill and Marg curled up on the couch to talk. It was nearly midnight when they decided it was time for bed.

"We'll need that beauty sleep, wouldn't you say?" yawned Jill. "Besides, I need to make a lunch to take along. I think we're going for a hike, and I said I'd make lunch. I'll need to do that before we leave. Short night coming up, Marg!"

They laughed.

"What a great start to the weekend. You know, Jill, I think I could really get to like Joe."

"We'll check that out more tomorrow. I've had it for tonight. Last one to sleep gets to make the lunch tomorrow," Jill challenged with a chuckle. "Just let me check to make sure I locked the door."

Yawning, they got ready for bed with high hopes for the next day.

Chapter 21

"Hey, sleepyhead. Rise and shine—breakfast at nine." Marg groaned and stretched.

"Remember, we're to meet the guys in town and bring along a lunch," Jill reminded.

Marg got up hurriedly. "Race you to the shower," she announced while pulling the covers off both of them.

"That's gratitude," Jill laughed. "Well, I'll start the sandwiches."

Soon, both girls were busy.

"I'm through with the shower. Your turn," Marg announced, toweling her hair. "I'll help make lunch. How about a coffee before we leave? I need a little jolt to really wake up for the day."

"There's the instant coffee and the kettle," Jill said, pointing as she headed toward the shower. "I've made sandwiches. We might want some carrot sticks and more of your cookies for lunch. And I'll get a blanket in case we need to sit on the ground. We'll buy cold drinks on our way."

By eight-thirty, the girls were ready and climbing into Marg's car.

"What a wonderful day to be out," Jill breathed. "It's so quiet you can almost hear the last leaves dropping to the ground. The sun is warm and bright, but the rays have a definite slant from the south now. I don't hear any more geese honking as they fly. One of these days it will snow, so I'm going to really enjoy this weekend."

"I was agreeing with you about the day, but you didn't have to mention snow," Marg said, pulling a face. "I must admit I don't enjoy winter with the icy roads, clearing the windshield before I drive, warming up the car… maybe I should learn to skate so I have a winter sport for fun."

"I'm hoping we can have a skating rink at the school," Jill mentioned. "That way, the kids can skate at noon and use up some energy. I could use the exercise, too."

Traffic was light, so they arrived at the restaurant early. Nonetheless, the boys were already there, watching for them.

"I think they're just as excited about being with us as we are to be with them," Marg confided happily. "You know, I think Joe is a great guy. Thanks for setting this up."

"Well, I really like being with Dan. I think we might get serious. But today is for fun."

The boys were already out of Dan's truck and heading toward the car.

"Going to sit there all day?" Dan teased, opening Jill's door.

Joe was heading for Marg. "With all that driving, you'll need a hand getting out," he joked as he helped her out.

Together, they all walked into the restaurant.

Jill slid into the booth first and Dan followed her. That left Marg and Joe on the opposite side, but they looked pleased with the arrangement.

"I hope you're hungry, since this place has a great breakfast option… bacon, eggs, toast, coffee—the works. We'll tank up here so that we won't be starving too early for our picnic." Dan looked at Jill. "You did bring a picnic lunch, didn't you?"

Jill laughed. "Yes. We brought sandwiches and cookies. We thought we could stop and buy cold drinks somewhere when we're almost ready to eat. Don't know how hungry you'll be by noon, so I hope it's enough."

"Should be. Especially after this big breakfast." Dan looked up as the waitress approached.

"Coffee?" the waitress asked.

"That would be great." Marg held out her cup and the others followed.

The waitress held her pen ready. "Ready to order?"

"Yup. Four breakfast specials," Dan answered for them all.

They took turns specifying toast and egg preferences, then started planning the day.

"We thought we'd hike along the river path this morning," Dan said. "Then we'll stop at the dam for a bit, walk across the train trestle, and picnic on the other side. Guess we'll have to buy our drinks before we cross. There's nothing but open land on the other side. How does that sound so far?"

"Great," they both assured him.

Dan looked to Joe. "Joe, you finish."

"Well, after we get back, it'll still be early enough to go bowling," Joe said. "Then we'll head to the A&W for burgers and fries and go out to Jill's to finish that Monopoly, or whatever we feel like by then. Do you have enough popcorn and hot chocolate, or should we buy refills?"

"Keep your popping arm ready," Jill said. "I have the corn and hot chocolate."

Joe glanced at the songs on the table jukebox. "Any favorites?" he asked, looking at Marg.

"'Oh Baby Mine,'" she answered quickly, then blushed as she thought of the words. *"Oh baby mine, I get so lonely when I dream about you…"*

Joe had already inserted a nickel and punched in her selection.

"Music, good company, and here comes the food. What more could we want?" Joe grinned.

After a leisurely breakfast, they all piled into Dan's truck. With four in the cab, it was close quarters, but none of them minded.

"Guess I'll have to drive with one arm again," Dan said. "You better learn to shift the gears." He glanced at Jill. "But I'll teach you on a country road, not here."

After they'd driven awhile, Dan wheeled into a parking lot.

"Hey, let's stop at the Bessborough Hotel," he said. "They have a great view of the city. We're not in a hurry and the day's activities aren't carved in stone."

They scrambled out of the truck and into the hotel's spacious lobby. Together, they strolled nonchalantly toward the elevator.

"What an impressive place," Marg said, looking around appreciatively.

Joe took Marg's hand. "It's a big place, and I don't want to lose you here."

After admiring the view, they sat a few minutes in some easy chairs, absorbing the stateliness of the place.

"Enough of this class," Dan said. "We're off to the river."

Dan jumped up and everyone followed.

"It was a fun stop. Thanks." Jill looked at Dan before they walked back out through the revolving doors.

They squeezed back into the truck and Dan took the street to the river.

"Everyone out," he said. "This is the start of the path."

Dan took Jill's hand and led the way. Marg and Joe followed. Although the leaves were gone from the trees, it was still a pretty path. Down the bank, they could see the river winding. The sun's rays warmed them as they strolled.

"This is such a peaceful path," Jill admired. "Not many people seem to walk here."

"No. I like to come here just to be quiet and think." Dan paused. "Having a quiet place to walk somehow helps me to think clearer."

"It's too quiet," Jill said after a while. "Where are Marg and Joe?"

They looked behind them.

"Well, the rascal!" Dan chuckled. "They've stopped to smooch. Here, I've been behaving so as not to embarrass them. Silly me." He put his arm around Jill. "Shall we? I've been wanting to do this."

Jill snuggled happily against Dan and put her arms around his neck.

It was several minutes before Marg and Joe caught up to them.

"Looks like wise minds think alike, eh, Dan?" Joe winked.

They bought drinks and headed to the trestle.

"Oh," Jill groaned, "the picnic blanket is in your truck."

"Not to worry. We're not camping. We'll just stretch out on the pasture and eat. There shouldn't be ants at this time of year."

The walkway was narrow. Halfway across, they heard the whistle of a train.

"Oh drat," Dan sighed. "A train. We're too far from either end to get off, so we'll have to press against the railing."

The engineer waved and then blew a deafening whistle blast as he passed.

"Guess that's our big excitement for the day," Dan said. "Let's hurry on over."

Once on the other side, they found a clear spot for lunch.

"What a perfect autumn day," Jill breathed. "This is such a high bank, you can see all the way up and down the river. Anyone want another sandwich or carrot?" Nobody took her up on the offer. "Well then, I guess it's time for more of Marg's cookies."

Joe smirked as he reached for a couple cookies. "I was a good boy and ate my carrots, so now I get dessert."

They left the last of the lunch for any stray birds or gophers that might be around and started the trek back across the trestle.

"Anyone ready for bowling?" Joe asked. "I think I'm ready to throw the ball straight down the lane."

"Talk is cheap. Wait until we get there!" Dan challenged as they headed to the pickup.

Chapter 22

"What a day. What a wonderful day! Breakfast out, roaming through the Bess, the hike and picnic, bowling, hamburgers and milkshakes for supper, and then here." Marg took a deep breath and slowly let it out. "I knew it would be a good weekend, but only in my wildest dreams did I think it would be this good."

Marg sprawled in an easy chair and hung her arms over the sides as she looked at Jill.

"I wish you could have seen Joe's face when you bowled two strikes in a row," Jill said. "It was priceless."

"Did he look mad? Disappointed?"

"More like proud, I'd say."

"Good. That should mean he won't be offended when I try my best." Marg sighed again. "I'm really glad we decided to include church in tomorrow's agenda. I have so much to be thankful for."

"Me, too," Jill added. "We can sleep in a little. The guys won't be here until ten-thirty. We don't have much work to do to prepare lunch. They're the ones who suggested soup and sandwiches. Tonight, I'm tuckered out. I'll say 'Goodnight, sleep tight.'"

"Don't let the bedbugs bite," Marg said, finishing the old rhyme.

They were soon both asleep.

It was Marg who woke first.

"Hey, Jill. Did we sleep in? What time is it?"

"Good grief. It's nine o'clock already. We'll have to fly through shower and breakfast."

"Coffee and toast are enough for me. Do you want first dibs on the shower?"

"Thanks. My hair dries a little slow." Jill headed for the shower. "Start the coffee, if you want."

Breakfast got the short order. Both girls spent time dressing and checking each other's hair and outfit.

"Made it with time to spare," Marg said plopping into an easy chair as she glanced at her watch. "Fifteen minutes to go."

Jill chuckled. "I wouldn't be so sure. I think I see Dan's truck coming up the road now."

"Got a spare cup of coffee for two thirsty bachelors?" Dan asked as he and Joe entered. "I think we have time."

Jill scurried for the coffee perk. "Sure thing. Do you want some toast with it?"

"Hey, why not? Thanks."

Joe and Dan pulled up chairs to the table.

"How about you, Marg?" Jill asked. "Want another cup?"

Marg laughed. "I'd never say no to a cup of coffee."

"You mean you can drink as well as bowl?" Joe asked appreciatively.

"That was a fun game. You guys really gave us a great day. Thanks." Jill looked around the table. "It's so nice to have people to share good times with."

"Amen to that," Dan said. "How long will it take us to get to church? Shall we walk or drive my truck?"

"Have you ever tried to walk in high heels, Dan? I'd really like a ride down that gravel road."

"Your wish, my command." Dan glanced admiringly at Jill. "We'll squeeze back in and try not to wrinkle your outfits."

It was a lovely Thanksgiving service. Jill was conscious of Sharon and Teresa peeking at her as she sat with her friends.

After the benediction, there were welcomes, handshakes, and some introductions.

"I'm so glad you all joined us today," Helen Gilmore said to them. Her smile was genuine. "It's great to have visitors."

"Marg and I went to Teacher's College together," Jill explained. "She teaches north of Saskatoon at Rosthern and came down for the long weekend. Dan and Joe both live in Saskatoon. We've had a lot of fun, but we all wanted to take time to give thanks this morning. It was a lovely Thanksgiving service."

"I confess that Stan spent a lot of time preparing so it would be meaningful. You four have a great afternoon." Helen smiled again and then moved on to welcome others.

Jill turned to go and found herself facing Sharon and Teresa.

"Hello, Sharon. Hello, Teresa," she said. "Wasn't that a nice service?"

Sharon and Teresa each nodded, but their gazes were on Dan and Joe. Their curiosity was evident.

Finally, inquisitive Teresa asked, "Which one is your boyfriend, Miss Jackson?"

Jill felt herself blushing. She could see that Dan was enjoying her discomfort.

"Well, girls, these are all my friends, but," she pointed to Dan, "this is a special friend."

Dan grinned.

Just then, Linda arrived. "You pestering your teacher?" she reprimanded slightly. "Good morning and have a great Thanksgiving weekend. It's great you could join us."

Linda took Sharon's hand and together they joined Howard. Teresa walked back to her folks.

Jill and her friends shook hands with Rev. Gilmore at the door before heading back to the truck.

"Hey, we're getting pretty good at this business of squeezing four into the cab," Dan said with a laugh.

"That was a nice bunch of people," Joe commented.

"I'm glad to see you have people like that for neighbors," Dan added. "I still feel some concern for you living alone out here."

"So far, so good. But I really do appreciate your concern, Dan. I'm careful. I lock my doors and—"

"Not this morning, you didn't," Dan interrupted. "I watched and we just all headed for the truck. Now I'll have to check to make sure no one's hiding in your closet!"

He looked at Jill and winked.

"Soup and sandwiches, here we come," he chuckled as they turned into the driveway. "Then we're off for a country drive."

"Sounds great," both girls agreed.

Jill glanced at Marg, who was snuggled against Joe. He had his arm around her shoulder.

Chapter 23

The day was perfect for a drive in the country. They ended up getting hamburgers and milkshakes before returning to Jill's place.

"What a wonderful weekend," Marg said. "I almost dread going back to the 'cage.' Well, actually, I enjoy teaching, so I'll get back into it. Christmas will be here before we know it. I may even come back for a weekend before that. That's what you get for giving me such a good time."

Marg glanced at Jill, then smiled at Joe.

"We'll count on that," muttered Joe. "I may even surprise you and drive up to Rosthern."

"That would be great," Marg said, beaming at the thought. Just warn me so I can bake some of those cookies."

"Why don't we go into town for a farewell breakfast tomorrow?" Dan suggested. "You bring Jill in, and I'll bring her back afterward. We'll see you off from Saskatoon. Your car will be at my place, so that will be handy for you, Joe."

Joe laughed. "You mean you don't want me helping you drive Jill back out here?"

Dan looked a little uncomfortable. "Whatever. You mentioned once that you had some work to do at the garage, and I thought you might be getting anxious to get at it."

"You're absolutely right." Joe smirked. "Breakfast tomorrow sounds like a good idea before farewells and work."

The guys gathered themselves up to say goodnight and affirm their plans for the morning.

Jill and Marg curled up on the couch to talk.

"Jill, I could really fall for Joe," Marg said after the men had gone. "I've had a great time with him. I kind of dreaded a whole weekend of a blind date, but this was actually an eye-opener. Now tell me, how are things really with you and Dan? I mean, it looks like you're made for each other. How do you feel?"

"I think if he asked me to marry him, I'd say yes in a moment. Maybe he'll ask at Christmas." Jill sighed and looked out the window. "I wish. Anyway, I just enjoy being with him and talking to him, and I'll enjoy it as long as it lasts. Maybe it will last a lifetime."

Marg looked over at her friend. "For your sake, I hope it does last a lifetime. For my sake, I need to know Joe better, but the way I feel after one weekend, well… time will tell. He's very special, I know that."

The next morning, Marg pulled her car into the restaurant parking lot beside Dan's truck and the girls hopped out.

Sliding into a booth beside a window, they each took a menu.

"Hey, I think we need some cheerful music," Joe offered. "This farewell breakfast is in your honor, Marg, so you pick the song."

"How about 'Oh What a Beautiful Morning'? Is that cheerful enough?"

"Suits me," Joe said, plunking a nickel into the table jukebox.

Tapping their fingers to the music, they chose their breakfasts just as the waitress stopped by to take their orders and pour them some coffee.

It seemed like only a few more minutes before their breakfasts came. Then it seemed like only a few minutes before Marg said reluctantly, "I'd better go. I really need to do some work before tomorrow. I left in such a hurry on Friday that I didn't do any lesson planning."

"I'll see you to your car," Joe announced. "That is, if Dan will let me out."

Jill started sliding out to let Marg get up.

"Come back soon," Jill invited.

"Thanks for everything," Marg said and turned to walk to the door.

"I guess it's not nice to watch, but I'm going to anyway," Jill said to Dan with a grin as the couple walked away. "It looks to me like this weekend lit a spark there."

"Pretty obvious, isn't it? I'm glad for Joe. He's a great guy."

They watched long enough to see Joe wrap his arms around Marg. Then Jill turned her attention to Dan.

"I suppose you have lesson plans to do, too?" Dan enquired.

"Yes. With so many grades in one room, there isn't much chance of winging it. I need to have things ready if I want to keep control. Mike is always pushing to see how far he can go with me or the kids. And Melissa…"

"Remember," Dan warned. "You can only do so much."

Jill nodded.

Joe came back in a few minutes later to split the bill with Dan, then made to leave. He didn't get very far before he turned to face them again, laughing.

"Either you have to take me with you to Jill's, or you have to take me to your place for my car."

Dan scratched his head. "You're right. My mind wasn't exactly on your car location when we made these plans."

"Hey, I don't bite," Joe said. "It's been a wonderful weekend, but I need to work this afternoon. If you're not staying at Jill's, I'll just come along for the ride… if you don't mind."

Dan agreed.

Even though there was more room in the cab this time, Jill snuggled against Dan. Joe looked out the window.

When they got to the teacherage, Dan jumped out and helped Jill out the driver's side. His kiss at the door sent her heart racing.

"See you soon?" she whispered.

"I sure hope so."

With a last squeeze, Dan turned back to his pickup and Jill went inside to try to put her mind on lesson planning.

Chapter 24

∾

"Guess I'll start work by making a cup of tea," Jill said aloud, trying to focus.

She brought her books to the table, poured herself a cup of tea, and sat down.

Moments later, she jumped up for the phone.

Who can be calling just now? Likely Mom. I should have phoned the folks this weekend.

Her quizzical "Hello" was met by Linda's cheerful voice.

"Hi, Jill. Is your company gone?"

"Yes," Jill said. "Marg had to drive up to Rosthern in time to do lesson plans. I'm starting the same thing here."

"I just wondered if you could come and have supper with us tomorrow night," Linda suggested. "Howie takes Sharon to music lessons after supper and you and I could visit."

"Well, I'd love to come. After this full weekend, I'm getting used to being with company." Jill laughed. "What time do you want me?"

"How about five-thirty? That way, Howie and Sharon won't be rushed to leave for Sharon's lesson."

"Great. I'll be there with bells on. Thanks for the invite."

Peanut butter and honey can wait another day! I know Linda is a good cook… but I wonder, is she finally going to tell me what's on her mind?

Jill settled into her lessons in earnest. When they were done, she phoned her folks.

"Where have you been all weekend?" Joanne asked, answering the phone accusingly. "Mom's been trying to get you. She's been worried."

"Mom knew I had a friend coming from Rosthern for the weekend," Jill defended. "Is Mom there now?"

"Where else would she be?" Joanne then called their mom to the phone.

Keep your cool, Jill. And please, Mom, don't tell me about all the wonderful things Joanne has done.

"Hi, Jill. How's it going?" Her mother's brightness sounded artificial.

"Great. Marg got down from Rosthern and it was a good weekend." Jill paused. "How's Dad? And how was your Thanksgiving?"

"Just wonderful," her mother bubbled. "Joanne baked the turkey and I made the veggies and pumpkin pie. Just three of us for dinner. I tried calling you."

"Sorry, Mom. We were on the go all weekend. I should have called sooner, but I thought you knew I had company."

"Well, yes, I knew. I would have asked you both to Thanksgiving dinner today."

"Marg had to leave early to get back to Rosthern, and I had to plan lessons for tomorrow, so dinner today wasn't possible. Thanks anyway. It's hard to get around without a car."

"You're right. I hope you can get one soon."

"Me, too. For now, I think I'll get ready for bed. Tomorrow will be here before I know it."

"Good night, Jill," her mom said. "Thanks for calling."

Jill hung up the phone slowly, then poured a bowl of cereal for supper and got ready for bed.

I miss Dad. It seems like he never answers the phone anymore.

On Tuesday morning, the kids were all geared up from their day off school. Jill started class by letting them talked about what they had done for the holiday.

Teresa said that her parents had driven to Medicine Hat to be with her grandparents. "Mom says I'm getting old enough to spend a couple of weeks there on my own this summer," she added proudly.

"You'll finish Grade Six this year," Jill replied. "Spending time with your grandparents sounds like a fun plan for the summer."

Larry said they had dug potatoes and put them in the cold room for winter.

Several other children told of their activities.

Jill looked at Melissa, but she was quiet.

"Time to get to work," Jill announced when everyone had talked who wanted to.

The class got out their books. Randy went to Ivan and started reading a book to him at the back of the class. Marie and Melissa sat working together on a book report. Honey flounced her way to the pencil sharpener in another new outfit. Butch came up to her desk to ask if he should take extra time tonight cleaning the room.

It was an interesting but uneventful day.

Four o'clock came and Jill was just as glad that school was over for the day as the kids were.

"Can I do the brushes and boards and then walk with you over to our house?" Sharon asked. She stood at Jill's side, pulling on a braid.

"Sure. You always do a good job and I appreciate it."

Sharon smiled and turned to gather up the chalk brushes.

Meanwhile, Butch was methodically spreading dust bane on the wooden floor and starting to sweep. After he finished each row, he moved the desks over so he could sweep where their feet had tracked in dirt.

"I'm glad you're the janitor here, Butch," Jill commended. "You do such a careful job."

Butch looked pleased. "I'm glad you're satisfied, Miss Jackson."

What a polite boy. I wonder if he'll be able to stay in school next year or if he'll have to drop out and help at the farm? I hope he can stay.

"Is there anything else for me to do tonight?" Butch enquired from the doorway, his cap in his hand.

"Thanks, Butch. That's all. Have a good evening."

"Night, Miss Jackson."

Butch carefully shut the door behind him.

Jill closed her books. "It's almost five o'clock, Sharon. How about we head out the door, too?"

"I'm finished the boards and brushes, Miss Jackson. It's nice that you're coming for supper."

Out on the gravel road, Jill took Sharon's hand. "Sharon, it's nice that your mom asked me."

Barely inside the back door, Sharon called out, "We're here!"

"I hope you don't mind that I'm early," Jill apologized.

"Mind?" Linda asked. "I'm glad. Sharon, wash up and you can set the table. Jill, I'll get you to mash the potatoes."

"Super." Jill washed her hands to help with dinner.

I feel so at home in this comfortable place. What a blessing it is to have Linda as my nearest neighbor.

Howard came in as Jill was mashing the potatoes.

"What's this?" he asked, raising his bushy eyebrows. "Putting our company to work?"

Jill laughed. "I'm not really company. I'm your neighbor, and I'm happy to say that I feel at home here."

Linda joined in. "I'm glad to have you as a neighbor. Maybe in the spring, you can have a garden patch here. We have lots of room."

"I've never had a chance to have a garden, but if I can grow carrots like you do, I'm sure willing to try."

"Supper's ready," Linda said. "Have a seat, everyone."

On the table was roast beef, mashed potatoes and gravy, mixed peas and carrots, a lettuce salad, pickles, and homemade brown buns. Jill's mouth was watering before the table grace was finished.

Howard offered the roast beef to Jill. "Help yourself."

"You won't have to ask me twice," Jill said, smiling as she took the platter.

Jill hadn't yet had a chance to talk to Howard, so she took the opportunity to ask about his farming.

"Wheat is my basic crop," Howard answered. "We keep cattle for milk and beef, and we sell a few for cash."

"I've got four chickens," piped up Sharon. "I have names for each of them. They lay eggs for us. They are *not*," she looked at her dad emphatically, "for frying."

"She's a little strong in her opinions," Howard admitted. "But she's mighty fond of those hens. And she takes good care of them."

The meal was soon over.

"Anyone for apple pie?" Linda offered.

"Why would you need to ask?" Howard observed dryly.

Supper finished, Jill exclaimed, "That was delicious. Sure beats peanut butter and honey!"

Sharon looked surprised. "Don't you cook, Miss Jackson?"

Jill smiled at Sharon and squeezed her cheek. "Sometimes. But sometimes it seems to take so long getting lessons ready for you kids that I take a shortcut on supper. That's when a sandwich comes in handy."

"Help clear the table, and then you can get ready for your lesson," Linda ordered.

Jill and Linda stacked the dishes ready for washing. When they were clean, Linda led the way into the living room.

"I sometimes feel the need to share something from my past," Linda began as they sat down. "So, make yourself comfortable. It could take a while."

Here it comes. I wonder what in the world is on her mind.

"I'll start with home. Mom wasn't affectionate. If I was helping her in the kitchen and happened to be in her way, she'd just give me a shove—or poke me with her knuckle. I don't recall ever getting a hug. Dad died in World War II, so I never knew him. Maybe Mom was lonely and didn't want to love again—even her daughter."

Linda shrugged her shoulders.

"When I met Abe," she continued, "you might say I was a little starved for affection. He was so kind, made me feel special."

Linda got a dreamy look in her eyes as she relived the memory.

"He told me I was the first girl in his life. He was certainly the first man in mine. I was eighteen and he was twenty-one… pretty heady stuff for a first love." She sighed. "Anyway, physical attraction is powerful. One night, when we were necking—too long, I know—he pressed a little. 'Don't you love me?' he asked. 'I want you so much.'"

Linda put her hand to her head.

"It wasn't the way I wanted to start making love. We were just in the back seat of his car, but by this time his pleading and my desire for him overcame my promise to myself that I would wait until the honeymoon for sex. Well, the experience was thrilling, but soon over. Then I had time to regret giving in, time to worry about whether I might be pregnant.

"The first month I missed, I thought it might just be tension or something. By the second month, I was getting nauseated in the morning. We were still dating. Finally, I found the courage to tell Abe that I thought I might be pregnant. He wasn't happy and he told me he wasn't ready to have a child. I reminded him that I wasn't, either. 'I'll pay the medical bills,' he told me, 'but the child is yours.'"

Jill was horrified. *How could a man profess love and then just leave after he produced a baby?*

"I was devastated," Linda said, again putting her hand to her head.

Jill reached out to hold the other hand.

"I had no options, Jill. I couldn't stay at home. I didn't have any way to support a child and keep a job. I carried the baby full term—a beautiful baby boy. I held him once before giving him up for adoption. I managed to get one picture."

Linda held up the worn picture of her baby boy, dressed to go out of her life.

"Just in case he ever tried to find me, to know why I gave him up, I embroidered my initials on the baby blanket I wrapped him in. I had sent word to Abe when I went to the hospital, but he never came. Never answered. He just paid the bills, as he had promised.

"I'll tell you this. A few moments of ecstasy are a high price to pay for a life of pain, of wondering where my boy is, of wondering if the adoptive parents are treating him right, of wondering if I'll ever see him in a crowd."

Linda paused. She and Jill sat quietly for a few moments.

"Howie came into my life a few months later," she continued. "He is a good, solid man. We had Sharon and I'm grateful to have a husband and child. But, oh Jill." It was almost a groan. "Regret doesn't alter what happened. I can see the light in your eyes when you speak of Dan. Please, don't forget my story. I share it with you to help you avoid the pain I still feel after nearly twelve years."

Jill took a deep breath. *I know too well how easy it might be at the moment to give in. What courage it took for Linda to share this poignant part of her past.*

"I can't imagine how difficult it was to tell me this," Jill finally spoke. "I want you to know that I really appreciate it. Your story might help me avoid the same pain. There are already times…" She paused. "I realize that once you're in high gear, it's almost impossible to put on the brakes. I'll be more careful to not get into high gear. Your story is too personal for me to repeat casually, of course. I'll keep it as a safeguard in my times with Dan."

Linda smiled and got up. "Let's have a cup of tea before Howie and Sharon get back. Then Howie can drive you home."

Linda went to the kitchen to heat the water.

They drank their tea in companionable silence.

"I hear the pickup now," Linda announced, and soon Howie and Sharon were at the door.

"Would you take Jill home?" Linda asked her husband. "It's getting pretty dark to walk."

"Sure thing," Howard said. "Tonight is chauffeur night, I guess."

Jill thanked Linda again and walked out.

Chapter 25

∽

The weeks raced by. Halloween was fun, with no serious pranks. Jill and Dan spent Remembrance Day sharing a meal, bowling, playing a game at her house, and enjoying each other's company.

Is he ever going to ask me to marry him? What's holding him back? Jill found herself getting a little anxious. *The time I spend with Dan is so special. Will it ever last a lifetime?*

On her way to school on Tuesday after Remembrance Day, the sky was overcast. Soon after she rang the bell, the snow started falling. Big fluffy flakes drifted out of the sky and soon piled up in the schoolyard. By noon, several inches lay on the ground.

"Oh, Miss Jackson," Marie said, sounding excited. "Let's go outside after we eat our lunches. There's enough snow to make snow angels."

Honey turned up her nose at the idea. "Too messy," she asserted.

But Sharon and Teresa were game to try, and Larry and Randy wanted to join the fun.

"How about you, Melissa? Will you come?" Randy invited.

Jill looked at Melissa, who was quite pale.

"I don't think so," Melissa said. "I feel sick, Miss Jackson. Can I stay in?"

"Of course, Melissa. Do you want to lie down?"

"No. I think I'll be okay. I'll just stay in through the noon hour."

How strange. She was fine this morning. In fact, she seemed to get sick at the thought of making snow angels. That's a strange reaction for a girl in Grade Three. Oh well, I guess it's just another piece of the Melissa puzzle.

The kids came in after lunch stamping their feet and waving wet mittens at each other. Jill was concerned about the snowfall. It was getting dark early and some of them had quite a ways to walk home, so she decided to dismiss them at the afternoon recess.

"Let's clean up around our desks," she said. "It will be dark soon, and with the snow falling this hard, the drifts will be quite deep for walking through. I'm going to dismiss you at recess. Is there anyone whose parents won't be home early?"

Honey's hand went up. "I think it's my mother's day to get her hair done."

"Well, you can stay here with me until four o'clock," Jill offered.

"Could I use your phone to call her? Maybe she'll pick me up."

"Certainly. We'll wait until everyone leaves, then go to my place to phone." Jill turned to Butch. "Butch, you can leave the sweeping tonight if you wish."

"I was wondering if I could shovel your sidewalk, Miss Jackson," Butch said. "The snow is getting heavy for you."

"What a kind thought. I'd be grateful if you'd clear the walk. Thanks, Butch."

The class hurried to get out the door. The deep snow seemed to be more fun for them than a problem.

Jill followed Butch as he shoveled a path.

"Would you like a hot chocolate before you leave?" she offered.

"Oh, thanks, Miss Jackson, but I need to make supper for Dad and me. You know my mom died when I was six. My dad does most of the outside work, although I help when I can. But I've basically turned into the cook. Maybe someday you'll come and see how well I do."

"Tell me the day, and I would be honored to come and taste your cooking."

Butch smiled and said goodnight. She could hear him whistling as he strode down the walk.

Honey soon finished her call. "Mom's home and will come and get me," she told Jill. "She doesn't want me to catch cold."

"She's right. We'll soon be getting ready for Christmas, and you don't want to be sick."

"Will we have a program?" Honey asked. "A program where we invite our folks?"

"I was thinking that would be a good idea. We'll talk about it tomorrow. Fresh snow just makes us think of Christmas, doesn't it?"

"We want to go to Vancouver for Christmas and see my grandparents. But Dad doesn't know what to do with Benjie. He's a purebred poodle and a little temperamental. Actually," Honey confided, "if a dog can be spoiled, Benjie is spoiled."

"I certainly hope you don't miss a Christmas vacation with your grandparents because you can't find a place for your dog," Jill replied emphatically. "Aren't there any kennels where you could leave him for a short time?"

"We're looking into it. Dad doesn't think Benjie would be happy in a kennel, so I don't know."

Jill glanced out the window. "That's your mom driving up now. I think that the snow will be too deep to drive in soon. Have you got your things?"

"Yes, Miss Jackson."

"Goodnight, Honey. It was nice talking to you."

Honey walked sedately to the waiting car.

Jill was starting to get supper ready when the phone rang.

"Hey, how are you doing out there? Snowed in yet?"

Jill smiled to hear Dan's voice. "Not yet. But I let the kids go at recess. With it getting dark early and so much snow falling, I decided not to keep them until four."

"Good idea. Do you need me to bring you anything?"

"You know you're always welcome, but I picked up enough groceries on Saturday to last me a few days. Thanks anyway. It's great to be able to pick something up every weekend. I'm even cooking supper now instead of relying on a sandwich."

"It's about time! Well, if you don't mind, I'll wait until Friday to come out. How about we come into town for supper? Maybe there's a show that's worth watching. I'll check."

"Sounds great." Jill paused. "Whatever we do, I enjoy being with you."

"What a coincidence," Dan said, chuckling. "I enjoy being with you, too. Or maybe you've noticed."

"I had a little inkling—and I'm glad."

Jill hung up and started her supper, thinking of Christmas plans to make the next day.

Chapter 26

∽

The next morning, the kids hurried in talking excitedly. Jill realized how fond she was of each one as she greeted them.

"I threw a snowball," Ivan announced proudly.

"Was that fun?" Jill enquired.

"Yeah, it was."

Jill patted Ivan on the shoulder. "Your English is really improving, Ivan. Good for you."

Larry stamped his feet on the steps and said, "Good morning, Miss Jackson."

Poor Larry. He always has a grubby smell. At least I still don't hear the other kids teasing him.

Honey and Melissa walked in together. Both girls were in Grade Three, but what a contrast there was between their lifestyles.

She greeted each of them.

"I saw lots of deer tracks," Mike gloated. "I'll soon get to go hunting with Dad. We eat venison most of the winter."

Jill went to her desk for opening exercises. When they had finished and resumed their seats, she said, "Christmas is coming. We want to put on a program for our parents and any grandparents who can come. This afternoon, we'll spend the last half-hour planning. Think of what you would like to do. If any of you would like to sing or play the piano or read a poem, be ready to volunteer. We'll have a Nativity. That's when we show the manger scene. Everyone can be in it. Some of you will be angels, shepherds, and so on. Now, let's get to work on our studies."

Randy stumbled a little as he headed for Ivan's desk. "Oops. Seems like I'm tripping on my own feet," he announced with a grin before sitting beside Ivan.

Ivan moved over to make more room and peered at the book Randy was holding.

Jill was surprised and pleased to hear Randy's suggestion. "This is your reader, Ivan. Why don't you read to me today?"

Soon everyone was working. Jill spent some time with each child.

Reading took up most of the time until recess. Mike Orlick did his best to read aloud from his reader, but when he said "steam" instead of "seam," even Jill had trouble keeping a straight face. It made the sentence quite humorous.

She sensed Mike's embarrassment and said, "Thanks, Mike. If you did that on purpose, it gave us all a chuckle-break from our work. But let's put our books away now. Time for recess. Don't forget to zip up your jackets!"

Jill sank into her chair and poured a cup of coffee from her thermos before looking over the math lessons for after recess.

When it was time to ring the bell, Jill stood up and walked to the door. Marie squinted up at her from the steps.

"Please may I ring the bell today?" Marie asked.

"Certainly, Marie. Thank you."

Jill stood aside as the kids came back inside for math.

By noon, she felt famished. The smell of sandwiches and banana and orange peelings soon filled the room as the kids opened their lunches.

"I'll trade you my banana for your cookie," Randy offered.

Teresa turned up her nose. "I had banana at breakfast."

"Anyone have a cookie to trade?" Randy asked everyone. No takers. "Guess I'll have to settle for banana." He bit the end to start peeling.

It would be nice to have a phone in the school, Jill thought to herself. *I'd call Linda and Helen and ask them over for a Coke and popcorn tonight. It will likely be too late after I get home after school. Why don't I think of these things sooner?*

Jill ate the last of her sandwich and looked at her watch.

"Hey kids," she said. "There's at least twenty minutes to play outside before we start class. Clean up your papers and get your jackets."

Honey groaned a little, but everyone else was eager to get into the sunshine.

After lunch, Jill continued reading *The Lion, the Witch, and the Wardrobe* to the class. She put her bookmark in just as Mr. and Mrs. Beaver were escaping with Peter, Lucy, and Susan.

"Do you think the white witch will catch them? Sharon, you've read the book, so please don't answer the question." Answers varied. "Well, we'll wait to see who guessed right. Now it's time for social studies."

A few minutes later, Jill was surprised to see Teresa standing at her desk.

Pushing her glasses higher up her nose, Teresa stood a little nervously on one foot, then shifted her weight to the other.

"Miss Jackson, I've been wondering…"

"Wondering what, Teresa?"

"Well, if you get married, will you still be our teacher next year?"

"Good gracious, Teresa." Jill noticed several heads looking in her direction and waiting for an answer. "I'm not even engaged and I really like this school, so it isn't a question I can answer." As an afterthought, she added, "Whatever made you ask a question like that?"

"Just wondering. Two years ago, our teacher quit in May to get married and we could hardly finish our grades."

"I can promise you this," Jill smiled. "Even if I got engaged, I wouldn't leave you in May. So, don't worry."

These kids are full of surprises. I'd have never dreamed they would wonder about me getting married. She sighed. *I'm the one who has the wedding dreams!*

When three-thirty arrived, she asked the class to close their books again. "Pick up around your desks and let's plan Christmas. What are your ideas?"

Sharon Martins raised her hand. "I could play a Christmas carol. I'll ask my piano teacher to give me a couple for my lesson next week."

"My mom makes special *rohalyki* for Christmas," Ivan volunteered. "I'll ask her if she'll make some for the concert."

"Ivan, that would be great. Thank you."

Marie raised her hand. "I sing in a kids' choir. Sometimes they ask me to do a solo. I could sing a Christmas carol."

"This is getting exciting!" exclaimed Jill. "Have any of you ever heard of 'choral speech'?" She heard lots of noes, and the kids' heads were shaking negatively. "Well, it will be hard for us to be a singing choir, so we can stand up and be a speaking choir. We'll learn the words to a carol like 'While Shepherds Watched Their Flock' and say it all together."

"Miss Jackson, why couldn't we draw pictures to hold up for each verse?" asked Melissa.

"Another great idea," Jill said. "We'll use art time to get those ready. Then, at the end, we can show the Nativity scene and the parents can sing 'Silent Night.' We'll need Mary and Joseph—Melissa, would you be Mary? You would just need to sit and hold a baby doll. Randy, would you stand behind her as Joseph? Then we'll need angels and shepherds. You girls can be angels—Sharon, Honey, Teresa, and Marie. Mike, Butch, Larry, and Ivan will be shepherds. We'll need to work on some costumes."

"Maybe we could get long white shirts to wear and tinsel for halos," Teresa suggested.

"Long shirts?" There was a definite note of sarcasm in Honey's voice.

"Everyone is entitled to an opinion," Jill said. "What would you suggest, Honey?"

No answer.

Jill sighed. "I know what. Just go home and talk to your folks about what you could wear. Likely the boys can borrow bathrobes and something for their heads. Girls, you talk to your moms. Maybe we could use white sheets and tinsel."

"What will I need, Miss Jackson?" Melissa sounded a little worried.

"I think I can lend you something," Jill reassured her. "Class, this is going to be great. We'll do it on Thursday evening, December 22, since some of you may be leaving after school on Friday to visit relatives during the holiday. We'll start practicing next week. Have a good weekend. I'll see you Monday."

And I'll see Dan in about an hour.

Chapter 27

Jill dressed carefully, just like she always did for Dan. She
pulled on a long blue wool skirt and a long-sleeved cream-
colored sweater. Then she pinned on the brooch Dan had
given her "just because." Vainly, she tried to smooth her cowlick
in the direction of the rest of her hair.

My hair has a stubborn streak—just like me, I guess. I'll just let it be.

She had a few minutes to wait until she heard Dan's truck
coming up the road.

*It's a good thing the grader did my driveway or he might have gotten
stuck.*

She smiled in spite of herself as she pictured trying to help
push the truck out of a drift or shifting gears while Dan pushed.

Jill got up as Dan walked in the door. Impulsively, she kissed
him hello.

"Hey, that's a good start to the evening," Dan said, laughing.
"You're looking good—as always. Maybe after we eat we can go
to a movie. Or we can come back here and relax."

Jill grabbed her coat and gloves. "Guess I better put on
boots. That snow is too deep for heels. I'd have cold ankles
before I walked far."

She grimaced a little as she pulled on the boots.

"It's better to wear boots than have cold, wet ankles," Dan answered practically.

Jill slid over to Dan in the truck and shifted the floorboard gears for him. It was already dark and the stars were starting to show.

Jill looked out through the windshield and commented, "I always like to see the sky… sunset, sunrise, sunshine with white clouds drifting, stars shining. It's always changing and always amazing."

"You're my poet," Dan said, giving her shoulder a squeeze. "Actually, you're making me appreciate the world around me more. I'm realizing how remarkable it really is."

They drove to their favorite restaurant in companionable silence.

"What'll it be tonight? I presume you'll want a change from peanut butter and honey," Dan teased.

Jill blushed a little. "Actually, I'm making more time to cook real meals. Things are settling in at school. Today we planned our Christmas program. We'll have it December 22, the day before holidays start. Maybe you'll be able to come out for it?"

"Your first Christmas program? I wouldn't miss it for anything. Maybe I can help set up chairs or something."

"Just having you there would calm my nerves." Jill laughed. "I'll probably have nightmares before the time arrives."

"You'll do fine. The kids will do fine. It's not a Broadway production, so enjoy it."

"You keep bringing me back to reality—and I'm glad you do." Jill smiled at Dan over her menu.

The waiter soon arrived.

"Pork chops for me and a Coke to drink," Dan ordered.

"The lady wants breaded veal cutlets and a pot of tea. We'll both have the baked potato. Am I right?"

"Right," Jill agreed. "And I'll have salad instead of soup for starters."

"Make mine the soup," Dan finished. "Thanks."

He reached across the table to hold Jill's hands.

"We might as well make good use of our waiting time," he said. "I love to hold these hands. I just think that, somehow, these hands do good things."

Jill was surprised and pleased at his thought. "Thanks. I hope you're right. I want to do good things. And I'm convinced that you do, too. That's part of your appeal."

The soup and salad arrived. Dan said grace, then reached for his soup spoon.

"How's your family?" Dan asked, out of the blue.

"Dad's health is failing some. I wish they could come out more, but Dad is getting so he doesn't like to drive on ice and snow. Mom keeps active by swimming every week. Joanne keeps busy at the store, and shopping, of course."

Jill smiled a little ruefully at the thought of Joanne.

"I should pick your folks up some Sunday afternoon and bring them out," Dan said. "How would that be?"

"That's very thoughtful. It would be great! I'll promise to cook a Sunday roast for dinner." As an afterthought, Jill added, "But I'd better wait until the New Year. December is getting full."

"Well, save time for a special dinner," Dan advised. "We'll make it New Year's Eve and go to the Bess for a celebration dinner. You've survived four months as a first-year teacher, with six months to go."

Is the celebration that I made it through four months of teaching, or will he propose that night? Or bring a ring? Whatever—it'll be special. We've only dated a few months. Quit rushing, Jill.

"Dinner at the Bess will be a real event," she said. "You can bet I'll save that Saturday."

"How about we just go back to your place, kick back, and drink hot chocolate tonight?"

"Sounds good to me." Jill reached for her coat. "Then I can get out of these boots. They're meant for cold weather, not for a warm restaurant."

They drove back slowly.

Once inside her house, Jill pulled off her boots and switched on a light. Then she lit some candles and flicked the light off.

"The lights seem to glare," she explained. "Candles have a soft glow."

"Agreed. And they're more romantic."

Jill paused. "I guess you're right."

"Now, don't tell me you didn't know that before?" Dan came up behind her, put his arms around her, and nuzzled her neck.

"I'll put on the kettle for the hot chocolate. Then we can sit and, as you say, kick back."

Jill could feel the romantic tension in the room as she put the kettle on the stove. She was excited and wary.

We're not even engaged. Be careful, Jill.

Chapter 28

❦

"Two hot chocolates, coming up," Jill announced as she came into the living room.

Dan had taken off his boots and sat slouched on the couch. He was curling his toes up and down.

"That's a new gym stretch," Jill said, laughing at the sight. "Now you can bend your elbow while you drink your hot chocolate."

Jill settled in beside Dan.

"What does your family do for Christmas?" she asked. "Do you open gifts Christmas Eve? Do you have a big gathering?"

"Whoa. One question at a time. We got out of the habit of a big celebration years ago. Mom and Dad don't even get a tree. Which reminds me… you need a tree here in the corner. Anyway, on Christmas Eve we go to church, then come home and have pie and ice cream. It's just Mom, Dad, and me, so opening one gift each doesn't take much time.

"We sleep in on Christmas Day, then get up late for French toast. Sometimes we go to my aunt and uncle's. Sometimes we have them over. There's no routine. Sometimes I loaf around or go visit friends. It's never a big group. How about you?"

"The four of us go to Christmas Eve service," Jill said. "When we get home, we light candles and tree lights and play Christmas records. We take turns deciding on our snack. Dad usually chooses Kentucky Fried Chicken. Mom has a favorite salad with raisin toast. Joanne and I either want nuts to crack or chips with a Coke to drink. We've drawn names for a gift, so we each open our gift on Christmas Eve. On Christmas Day, the four of us have a turkey dinner. Pretty bland."

"Maybe we can liven things up a little," Dan suggested. "You could come to our place Christmas Eve and I'll go to your place for turkey dinner. Any chance of pumpkin pie?"

Jill laughed. "You're really taking a chance, but I could try to bake one."

Jill took their empty mugs to the kitchen and came back snuggling against Dan. It was so cozy sitting and talking about family and Christmas.

In a moment, Dan had his arm around her and his lips on hers. They exchanged tender kisses at first, but as he pulled her closer, the kisses became more passionate.

"Jill, Jill."

He was breathing heavily and drawing her closer.

Jill felt her heart pounding. The ecstasy of being in Dan's arms was clouded by her desire for restraint. She thrilled as she felt Dan's hand sliding down her abdomen.

If we don't stop now, we won't be able to. Lord, what do I do? I love this man.

"A few moments of ecstasy are a high price to pay for a life of pain."

As clearly as if Linda was in the room, Jill heard the words. She pulled back.

"Dan," she said, feeling miserable. "I don't want to start sex as an out-of-control and unplanned event. I want to look forward to giving myself to you, to have the blessings of the marriage ceremony. Isn't that what you want, too?"

Dan's head dropped. "Yes. I've always meant to save myself until I was sure of my love, then give myself to my bride. You're right. I would have gone all the way and then been disappointed in myself. You're the first girl who has almost made me lose my determination." He paused. "I'll leave for tonight, to give us both time to cool down. And thank you. I know that took courage. You were just as hot as I was."

He laughed ruefully.

"I'll call tomorrow," he said. "Maybe we can go bowling."

Dan got his coat and boots, gave her a quick hug and kiss, and was gone.

Chapter 29

∾

Jill woke Saturday morning with mixed feelings.

I love that man. I want to be with him. It was so hard to stop, but I think we both feel better for waiting. I'm so glad he didn't push me. I wonder when he'll call.

Jill stretched and got up. She was just getting her coffee when the phone rang. Sprinting back to the phone, she managed to keep most of her coffee in her mug until she set it down.

"Hi, Jill." It was Linda. "Want to go shopping today? I'm just going in for groceries and back."

"Sounds good. We can visit on the way. I just need to make a quick phone call, but I can go. What time?"

"How about twenty minutes?"

Jill thought of her messy overnight hair. "If you saw me now, you wouldn't think I'd make it, but I'll do my best!"

Linda laughed. "Okay. If you still look like a monster in twenty minutes, I'll wait."

Jill clicked off with Linda. She started to call Dan next, then paused.

He may still be sleeping. He knows I often go shopping with Linda Saturday morning. I'll get ready to go. Just in case he happens to come out here, I'll leave a note on the table.

Jill scribbled her note, then hurried to the bathroom to try to fix her unruly hair.

Twenty minutes later, she sank into Linda's car. "Made it! Just call me the original quick change artist! If you had seen me when you called…" Jill rolled her eyes and groaned. "Where's Sharon?"

"She had to practice her piano. Says she's playing at the Christmas program. How are things going for the program?"

"I'm excited," Jill said. "By the way, do you know about the Kolisnyk family? Ivan offered to have his mom make special Ukrainian Christmas cookies. It would be great, but I'm concerned whether the cost will be a problem for them. He was so excited to make the offer."

"I'm not sure. They haven't been here long." Linda mulled the situation over for a few minutes. "Why don't you drop by their house? Take ten dollars. The school board has some funds for petty cash. Say the Ukrainian word for the cookies and offer her the money."

"I could try." Jill sounded doubtful. "I wouldn't want to insult her."

"Look. I'll try to ask around and see if it would be a hardship for them to buy the ingredients. They may just want to do this to be part of the community. Not knowing English hampers them from participation in other ways."

"Thanks, Linda. What would I do without you?" Jill paused. "I owe you a lot."

"Nonsense. What are friends for?"

"I mean in another way. I may have had a lifetime of regret if you hadn't shared your story with me. Last night, I could hear your voice saying, 'A few moments of ecstasy are a high price to pay for a lifetime of pain.' That made the difference.

We were able to put on the brakes. I cannot say what would have happened if you hadn't warned me. I am truly grateful to you."

Linda reached over and squeezed Jill's hand. Soberly, she said, "Well, that's one good thing that came from my experience."

Shopping didn't take long and they were soon pulling back into Jill's driveway.

"That's Dan's truck," Jill exclaimed. "Good thing I wrote him a note. Anyway, thanks, Linda."

She pulled her bags from the car and headed to the house.

"Welcome home!" Dan greeted when she stepped inside. "What have you got that's good for lunch?"

Dan reached for her bags and started putting things away as she took off her boots.

"It's a good thing you wrote that note. I might have thought you'd run away." Dan grinned at her. "I brought a peace offering. Look in your living room."

"Oh, Dan, they're gorgeous," Jill whispered, looking at the bouquet. "Thank you. Thanks for everything." She turned and kissed him. "What's good for lunch, you ask? How about soup and a grilled cheese sandwich?"

"Great. Then we'll go bowling. I have to be home for supper. I forgot that it's Mom's birthday."

Dan stirred the soup. "This is my first cooking job here. I better not let it burn."

"If you burn the soup, I'll burn the sandwiches!" Jill laughed as she turned the sandwiches in the pan.

Lunch was pleasant. They visited easily, the same as all the other times before the previous evening's near-miss.

A chickadee perched on the bush outside the kitchen window.

"I'd better get some suet to put out," Jill said. "That little guy comes here quite often."

"We can pick some up after bowling. You'll need something to lift your spirits after I make at least three strikes."

"You're on. Besides, you'll be lucky to get even one today. I'm going to aim at that center pin and get a couple strikes myself!"

Dan held Jill's coat and they walked to the truck. "Let's go find out who's just talking."

Jill glanced at Dan while she slid in beside him. "I think I can still switch the gears for you."

"I don't think I can manage them alone anymore," Dan answered with a smile.

"It's nice just to get out and go somewhere. You've made a huge difference in my life out here."

"How are the plans for the Christmas program? Need any help?"

"Everything is falling into place. I'd be glad if you'd put up chairs for the parents. Mingle a little. But the kids are really getting into it. They've got ideas for decorating and drawing pictures. Ivan has offered for his mom to make Ukrainian cookies. They sound delicious—if I understood him right. Melissa will be Mary in the Nativity scene, while Randy will be Joseph and the other kids will be angels and shepherds. Everyone's taking part in different ways."

Dan squeezed her shoulder. "Looks like you have it all under control. I'm proud of you. And at the bowling alley, you can be proud of *me*." He laughed at his own challenge.

Jill slid out of the truck when they arrived. "Pretty sure of yourself, aren't you?"

"Not as sure of myself as I used to be." Dan took her hand as they walked across the parking lot.

I won't ask, but I think I know what he means.

Chapter 30

"Whoa, Dan. You had a strike already," Jill protested with a smile as he slid into the seat beside her. He grinned. "I told you I'd make three today."

"Just wait until the game is over."

Jill picked up a returned ball, felt its weight, stepped back, then ran lightly up to the stop line. Unfortunately, she lost her balance a little as she let the ball go and it rolled into the gutter.

"Well, I'll try for a spare." She tried, but missed the final pin. "Not my day—yet."

Jill let her third ball go and watched the last pin fall over.

"Well, at least I got fifteen." She slid in to mark her score while Dan strolled over to pick up a ball.

"Another strike!" Jill marveled once he finished throwing. "I can't believe it." She walked up and picked another ball. "Maybe this one will be a little lighter."

"Hey, you should try ten-pin bowling," Dan teased. "Now those balls are heavy."

"I'll settle for five-pin, thank you."

Jill took careful aim this time, just to the left side of the middle pin.

"Whee. That's more like it," she exulted with the resulting strike.

When they finished the game, Dan asked, "Want another game? We have time."

"I'm okay to wait for another day. You don't want to be late getting to your mom's. Wish her a happy birthday for me." As an afterthought, she added, "You can eat my piece of cake, too."

"One of these days I'll take you there to eat your own cake. Mom's a good cook. Dad's a little cranky these days." Dan paused. "He had an argument with a brother and they've never sorted it out. Now he seems to have a chip on his shoulder for anyone who crosses him."

They headed to the truck and got in.

"You're getting pretty good at shifting these gears," Dan said, smiling at Jill and squeezing her shoulder with his right arm.

"I had a good teacher." Jill slid into third while Dan held the clutch pedal down. She glanced out the window. "You know, the evergreen trees look so nice with snow on their branches. No decorations needed."

"That reminds me," Dan said. "We need to get a tree to perk up your living room. Do you think your folks have any extra decorations?"

"I'll ask. It's getting so they aren't so interested in decorating for Christmas anymore, at least not with just four adults to admire things. But I love to sit with only the lights on and Christmas carols playing."

"Me, too. You definitely need a tree," he said. "And never mind asking your folks for decorations. We have lots—I'll bring some when I come. We'll get your groceries Friday after school.

Saturday, I'll pick you up and we'll go tree hunting. It would be more fun to find a place to cut down our own."

Dan looked thoughtful.

"I think I know a place we might be able to cut one down," he continued enthusiastically. "We could take a thermos of hot chocolate, pick our tree… well, I'd better check before we make all the plans."

"It definitely sounds like fun."

They pulled into the driveway. Dan walked Jill to the door.

"Enjoy the birthday dinner," she told him. "I know my folks tell me how they love to have me home for special meals… or any other time. I'll bet your mom is the same."

"You're a sweetheart," Dan whispered as he kissed her goodbye. "I'll give your birthday wishes to Mom."

Jill unlocked her door and went in to switch on the light. Dan headed for the truck. Somehow, the house always seemed extra quiet when Dan left.

Jill put on the kettle for tea and wondered what to have when suppertime came.

On an impulse, she picked up the phone and dialed home.

"Hello?"

What a pleasant surprise! Dad had answered.

"Hey, how are you?" she asked. "What are you up to? Is your arthritis acting up with the cold?"

"Same old Jill," he said. She could hear her father's smile. "More questions than I can shake a stick at. I'll answer your last question first, and the answer is yes. My leg is getting pretty gimpy in this weather. That means the answer to your second question is I'm sitting around the house wanting to be doing things. That's how I am."

Her dad finished with a brief sigh.

"But tell me what you're up to," he said. "Seems like too long since I've seen your cheery face. And even longer since I held you on my knee. But I'm getting mushy in my old age."

"Oh, Dad, I love you. You can mush all you want. I remember being on your lap with one arm around me and one holding a book to read. What wonderful memories. You'd let me turn the pages and I'd pretend I could read them!" Jill smiled at the memory and then continued, "Dan said he'd bring me in for Christmas. I know you don't want to do winter driving anymore."

"No. I feel a little nervous, always watching for an icy patch. But this Dan you keep mentioning… is he pretty special?"

Jill always felt comfortable talking to her dad.

"Well, he's special, all right." She thought a moment. "Even if nothing comes of our friendship, he'll be part of special memories."

But I sure hope something comes of it… that the special memories are shared.

"He'd like to come over to our house Christmas Day. Then you'll meet him."

Dad chuckled. "I'd like that. I'm a pretty good judge of men. I'll check this guy out and see what I think of him dating my daughter."

Somehow the idea pleased Jill. She was sure Dan would get her father's approval, but it would be nice to hear her father actually say that he approved of Dan.

"Right. You can check him out for me," she said. "Anyway, I put the kettle on and it's going to boil dry if I don't take it off soon and make my tea. Say hi to Mom. It's so good to talk to you, Dad. Give me a call sometime."

Jill hung up the phone, made her tea, and settled into her easy chair with her feet up.

Chapter 31

Jill jumped when the phone rang, almost spilling her tea.

"Hey, Jill. What's up?"

"Marg… it's great to hear your voice. The only thing up here is my feet. They were on the hassock. What's going on? Are you planning to come down?"

"No. Joe's coming up this weekend. He's been up three times now. Jill, I'm a goner. If he proposes, I'll say yes and try not to dance a jig to celebrate. And it all comes from you having me down for Thanksgiving weekend. I'd have never dreamed…"

Marg gave a low whistle and waited for Jill.

"Well, I'm a goner too, as you put it," Jill said. "But Dan hasn't said anything about getting engaged. I just know I love to be near him."

Jill paused a few moments, then changed the subject.

"Anyway, are you coming down for Christmas and New Year's?" Jill asked. "I think I'm going to Dan's for Christmas Eve, but it would be fun to do something together for New Year's Eve."

"Joe has asked me to come down. I'm not going to try to go home to my folks' place. It's too far for winter driving.

Can I stay at your place during the holidays? You're likely going to be in Saskatoon. Would your folks mind if I stayed there a few days?"

"Oh, Marg, they'd love it. They ask about you sometimes, since you came to the house when we were in Teacher's College. Plan on it."

"Thanks, Jill. Better sign off. My three minutes are nearly up. Take care!"

That makes the holidays sound like a lot of fun, Jill told herself when she hung up. *We'll plan something special for New Year's Eve.*

Jill went back to her easy chair, put her feet up again, and took a sip of lukewarm tea.

The phone rang again.

"Boy, this is my night for phone calls," she announced to herself.

It was Dan.

"Hey, Jill, guess what?"

Dan sounded exuberant. Before Jill could even venture a guess, he went on.

"I just checked with a buddy whose folks own a farm near you. They have evergreens and wouldn't mind if we cut down a small one. Bundle up Saturday and make a thermos of hot chocolate. We're going to find that tree."

"Oh, that sounds like fun. I'll make some cookies to go with the hot chocolate."

"Cookies? Since when are you baking?"

"Since I have a reason—it's no fun to bake for just myself."

"Have it your way. Have you got some high boots? The snow might be deep in the pasture."

"Just my ordinary boots that come up over the ankle," Jill answered, disappointed.

"Not to worry. I'll bring some heavy socks. You can pull them up over your jeans. That should keep you fairly dry. I haven't looked in the woods for a Christmas tree since my dad used to take me out when I was a kid. I loved it then."

"It's a deal," Jill said. "I've never gone to actually cut down our own tree. What time do you want to leave?"

"I was thinking you might want to make bacon and eggs around nine and then we'd leave on our expedition."

Jill laughed. "Bacon and eggs, cookies and hot chocolate. You got it. You've got the truck and the axe, so we're set."

"Do you think you have a pail we can set the tree in?" Dan asked. "We've got some bricks here that will hold it steady and let us water it."

"I'll have a pail by Saturday. Maybe Linda or Helen have an extra one. I'll find something."

"See you Friday for shopping. Be sure bread is on your shopping list, so we can have toast Saturday morning."

"I'll add toast to your menu order," Jill said with a laugh. "I might even put on some jam!"

"Good idea. My sweet tooth needs a fix. See you soon."

Jill could hear Dan chuckling as he hung up.

Chapter 32

∾

Thursday seemed like a long school day. The sky was gray and overcast from one horizon to the next. Soft, white snowflakes fell. The temperature was close to zero degrees. Butch busily kept the fire going in the big central stove.

They followed the timetable for the morning. After lunch, Jill finished reading *The Lion, The Witch, and The Wardrobe*. They discussed the story. Some kids commented on the death of Aslan in place of Edmond being like Jesus dying in our place. Others mentioned Lucy riding on Aslan's back to the witch's castle being exciting.

Jill let them talk until recess.

"Time to go out and get some fresh air," she announced.

Honey sniffed a little. "Do I have to? The snow might go over the top of my winter boots."

"Just keep out of the deep snow," Jill advised. "A few minutes outside will wake you all up. After recess, we'll work on our Christmas program. We want to do a good job when your families come."

It took nearly fifteen minutes for the kids to get into their wraps and boots and get outside. Soon they were whooping, dropping into the fresh snow, sticking out their tongues to catch snowflakes, chasing each other, and generally having a good time. Jill smiled. She enjoyed watching them have fun together.

While the kids played outside, she got their pictures together for the practice time after recess, then picked up the bell. The kids tramped in with rosy cheeks, stamping off the snow before taking off their boots.

Larry and Ivan came in together. They were the two youngest boys and Jill was pleased to see that they were starting to play together. Ivan's English was improving, and it was becoming easier for him to talk to a friend.

Mike managed to fake a trip and bump into Teresa, who gave him a glare. Jill decided to ignore the incident.

Soon the kids were in their desks.

"Now, let's see how we're doing," Jill said. "Sharon, do you have a piano piece ready to play?"

"Yes," Sharon said. "I'm going to play 'Joy to the World.' Two verses."

"Great. That's a happy carol. Maybe you could play it for us on Monday for practice." Jill turned to Ivan. "Ivan, is your mom going to make the *rohalyki*?"

"Yeah," Ivan answered excitedly. "You will like them."

"That's great. It will be special to have a Ukrainian treat at Christmas," she said. Ivan beamed at her. "Marie, what song are you going to sing?"

Marie looked suddenly bashful. "Our choir is practicing 'O Little Town of Bethlehem.' Would it be okay if I sing that?"

"It's one of my favorite carols," Jill said, smiling. "How would it be if you sing on Monday, after Sharon plays the piano? That will give you some extra practice." As an afterthought, Jill asked, "Do you want me to play the piano while you sing?"

Marie looked relieved.

"Good," Jill said. "We can practice at noon tomorrow. Bring

your book along." She turned her attention to the rest of the class. "Now, let's practice reading 'While Shepherds Watched Their Flock.'"

The class got out their books and read the lines together.

When they had finished reading, Jill advised, "That's good, but we need more variety in your voices. If you older boys can lower your voices and if some of you girls can speak in a higher tone, that would be splendid. Let's try it again."

After another few minutes of practicing, Jill noticed some improvement. *This is new to them. What else can we try? Maybe a solo part would add interest.*

"Randy, could you talk loud enough to read a part alone? I'd like you to say the words the angel says in the song."

"Sure, Miss Jackson," Randy said with a grin. "I'll try not to drop my book."

"That would mess things up," Mike growled.

"I'll underline the part for you to say and we'll practice at recess," Jill said. "Now, get your illustrations and we'll stand up and go over this one more time."

Jill helped them find a place to stand with the younger students together at one end and the older students at the other end.

"Oh, class. You're doing so well," Jill praised after they finished. "Your parents will be proud. They can bring friends if they want."

Jill motioned them to their desks.

"Now, how about costumes?" she asked. "You'd better bring them tomorrow so we can make sure we have enough. I bought tinsel for the angel halos. Melissa, I found your outfit to wear as Mary."

Before she knew it, the day was over.

"Good gracious. It's nearly four o'clock! Pick up under your desks and get ready to go home. It gets dark early now and I don't want you out on the roads after dark."

She waited a few moments until they were ready.

"Hurry home, kids. I want you home before dark," she warned before dismissing them.

Jill sank into her chair and looked at lesson plans while Sharon cleaned the boards and Butch swept the floor.

"Goodnight, Miss Jackson," Sharon said from the door.

"Oh, goodnight, Sharon. Thanks again for helping. I'm looking forward to hearing you play your piece on Monday."

Sharon smiled and stepped outside.

"Anything else, Miss Jackson?" Butch asked.

"No thanks, Butch. I really appreciate the cleaning you do here. Have a good evening. Are you the chef tonight?"

Butch smiled. "Yes. Dad won't get home until after six."

"I'm sure your dad is grateful to come home and have dinner ready."

"That's what he says. I don't mind cooking. Maybe I'll get a job as a cook one day."

"I hope you can stay in school next year," Jill said, looking at Butch. "I know it's tough going to school and helping on the farm, but I really hope you can manage at least one more year."

"Well, we'll see. I'm not sure yet." Butch hesitated. "I'd better get going if I'm going to have supper ready. Goodnight, Miss Jackson."

"Goodnight, Butch. Thanks again for cleaning up. You are so dependable." She smiled at Butch as he turned to get into his winter clothes and leave.

I wonder what I'll have for supper tonight. I'd better go home before it gets any darker. Sometimes walking through that hedge in the dark gives me the willies.

Jill gathered up some work to take home, locked the schoolhouse, and headed up the path.

"That's the phone," she announced happily to no one when she heard the familiar ringing. She sprinted down the path to the kitchen door.

Once inside, she grabbed the phone. "Hello?"

"You don't know it's me yet, and still you're breathless," Dan teased. "Anyway, good news for Saturday. I'll bring the axe, some wieners and buns, and stuff for a fire. You can take it from there. Now, this is only a suggestion, you realize," he paused dramatically, "and I'm not telling you what to do…"

What in the world is he suggesting? Get on with it!

"May I suggest two thermoses of hot chocolate, some marshmallows, mugs, relish and catsup for the hot dogs—and something you dream up for dessert?"

"May I suggest," Jill replied, "that you've thought this over carefully and I'll be glad to follow your suggestions?"

They both laughed.

"Oh, Dan. It sounds like so much fun. A winter wiener roast and a fresh tree we cut ourselves. I can hardly wait. What time do you want me to be ready Saturday?"

"Don't tell me you forgot the bacon and eggs at nine," Dan said, attempting to sound grieved. "We'll leave at about ten o'clock. It will be warming a little by then. Should be a nice day, according to the forecast—and according to our plans. I'll still pick you up Friday for a quick grocery shopping expedition." He paused. "By the way, how's the Christmas program coming along?"

"We practiced today. We'll keep working on it next week and have it ready by Thursday night. I'm content. They'll do their best and it will be a good evening with the parents coming."

"Atta girl. Having the program and the parents is the important thing. Not perfect speeches."

"I'm glad you're coming," Jill said. "But I shan't think of the program Saturday. Saturday is definitely for fun."

"You bet. See you then. Hey, have a good evening and don't work too hard."

I'm glad he didn't ask what's for supper. I think I'll open a can of soup and make a sandwich. If the way to a man's heart is through his stomach, my suppers aren't much of an advertisement. I'll have to look for a good dessert recipe for Saturday.

Jill opened a can of soup, put a piece of cheese between two slices of bread, and waited for the soup to heat.

The phone rang again.

Busy place. Two phone calls in one night!

Jill reached for the phone.

"Hi, Jill. It's Helen. How are the plans for the Christmas program? Can I help?"

"I'd love to have you come over tomorrow around three o'clock," Jill said. "The kids are supposed to be bringing their costumes and it would be great to have help trying them on and seeing if we still need anything. And thanks for the costume for Mary. Melissa will look sweet in it."

"Hey, I like helping out for kids' programs. How would it be if I came over tonight so we can go over things together?"

"I'll put the kettle on," Jill said happily. "I'd love for you to come. Winter nights are a little long—and sometimes a little lonely."

It's amazing how the thought of company perks me up. Even the soup looks more appealing!

Jill finished supper and started singing "Jingle Bells" as she cleared the table and laid out store-bought cookies for tea with Helen.

Next week at this time, we'll be having the program. I hope it goes well. The kids are really into it and most of the parents are coming. Only Steve Webber seems like a puzzle. He kinda gives me the creeps. But I hope he comes, for Melissa's sake.

Helen arrived and they went over the program.

"We have a Ditto machine. Do you want to make up printed programs?" Helen offered.

"That sounds really special. I'll prepare an outline. Maybe Melissa could add a border or a drawing. She's really artistic—but rather shy and withdrawn. She concerns me."

Helen looked thoughtful. "Her dad used to be a boxer. Looks tough. Her mother looks… too quiet. Nobody visits their place—they don't welcome visitors."

"I learned that when I walked toward their house one day. Steve Webber came along the road and informed me it was a dead end. I never walked that way again—only toward the Martins' place and the church."

"You're probably wise not to push him," Helen said gravely.

"Now, time for tea. Would you like store-bought cookies or cinnamon toast? Your choice." Jill smiled and shrugged. "Sorry, but I have nothing else to go with our tea."

"Let's try the cinnamon toast. I haven't had that in ages."

Jill put the kettle on and mixed some cinnamon and sugar.

"Where are your teabags?" Helen asked. "I'll watch the kettle while you make toast."

They soon settled in the living room with tea and cinnamon toast.

"On Saturday, we're going out to get a tree for my living room. I think that will make it so cozy."

"By 'we,' I'm guessing you mean the guy you brought to church a couple of times. How's that going?"

"Yes, I mean Dan. I think it's serious. We have a great time together. Guess I'll just have to wait and see what happens, but I'm going to enjoy Saturday and the tree fetching. The tree thing is all his idea, but it'll make the place more festive."

They talked a while longer, then Helen said she needed to get home. "If I stay too long, the car might freeze. We have to plug it in when it's cold like this."

Jill laughed. "That's a problem I'd like to have."

Helen put on her wraps, found her car key, and turned the doorknob.

"Don't forget to lock the door," she admonished and waved goodbye.

Chapter 33

∽

Saturday morning was crisp with brilliant sunlight dazzling on the new snow. Jill scurried around the kitchen setting the table, impulsively putting her poinsettia plant out for decoration, and finding pretty napkins. Next, she worked on her hair, trying to settle her troublesome cowlick and tucking in some curls.

That'll have to do, with jeans and a warm sweater under my jacket. Time to start the coffee. This will be a great day.

She had barely started the coffee perking when she heard Dan's truck.

He's usually early and I'm often slow. What a pair we make!

"Coffee coming up," she announced as he came blustering in the door. "I forgot to ask how you want your eggs."

"Easy over would be great."

She stood over the frying pan. The bacon was starting to sizzle and the aroma filled the kitchen.

"This is living," Dan said as he settled into a chair at the table. "Hmmm, I think I smell the coffee." He ambled over to the perk and poured a cup. "Want a cup while you fry?" He smirked at the wording of his question

"I'll wait and keep the coffee hot."

Jill put the bacon on a plate lined with a paper towel to soak up the extra fat.

"You can start the toast," she said. "I'm ready to fry the eggs. Two or three?"

"I'll take three. You'd better have at least two. It's cold out and we'll have to walk a little."

Dan put the toast in. Soon they were both at the table.

"Beautiful day to be out in the woods," Dan commented. "And a beautiful day to sit at breakfast before we leave."

"I'm excited," she told him. "I've never done anything like this before. Cutting a tree, a wiener roast in the snow—it just sounds like so much fun."

"You know what's fun about a small table like this?"

"No—I can't guess. But you have that mischievous look."

"Well, you can play kneesies."

"What in the world is 'kneesies'?"

"Oh, it's easy to learn. It goes like this." Dan dropped his knee against Jill's and rubbed a little.

Jill laughed. "Even I can learn an easy game like that." She rubbed Dan's knee against hers.

"Want more coffee?" She jumped up to pour. "By the way, did I tell you Marg phoned? She's coming down for Christmas. Looks like she and Joe really hit it off at Thanksgiving."

"Yeah, Joe's been talking. He's been up there a few times now. They look like a good match and I'm glad for them both. Guess we did a good deed setting them up."

"Well, Marg sounds happy."

"Okay, it's nearly ten o'clock," Dan said. "How about we get our happy twosome out to the truck? Can I carry anything?"

"I've got it all tucked in here." Jill lifted a cooler with the mugs and goodies and handed Dan the two thermoses.

They slid into the truck and started up the road.

"What a magnificent day," she said. "The fresh snow looks so clean and I love when the sun shines on it. Look at the tree branches—the snow is still stacked on them. How much snow fell last night?"

"About two inches," Dan replied. "But I think it'll be quite deep in the fields. Too bad we don't have snowshoes."

"Have you ever tried them?"

"Once. It wasn't too bad, at least not until I stepped one snowshoe on the edge of the other and fell on my face in the snow." Dan chuckled at the memory. "It was pretty cold when the snow slipped down my neck and under my shirt."

Jill laughed.

"Here we are," Dan said as he pulled off to the edge of the road. "I told you it wasn't too far. We'll leave our lunch here and walk over to find a tree."

Dan reached into the back of his truck and hefted an axe onto his shoulder.

Together, they waded through the snow-filled ditch, heading toward the trees.

"Careful here." Dan held two strands of barbed wire apart so Jill could crawl through.

"Thanks. Let me hold it for you."

Dan crawled through carefully.

"Pretty good, I'd say. Neither one of us got hooked."

They continued on across the field, looking for just the right tree. They laughed as they accidentally dislodged clumps of freshly fallen snow from the branches. It would land on their parkas and they'd shake it off and head into another dump of snow.

"How about this one?" Dan pointed to a tree. "It's just about your height."

His eyes measured Jill and the tree.

"It has nice thick branches—a good choice."

Jill watched as Dan swung his axe.

"Looks like you've done this before," she commented.

"Boy scouts taught us quite a bit about the outdoors. That might be part of the reason I enjoy being out so much," Dan said. "There. That should do it."

He gave a little shove and the tree toppled over.

"You carry the axe," he said. "Be careful, it's sharp. I'll carry the tree."

Dan put the stump over his shoulder and let the tree trail behind, its top dipping into the snow.

When they got back to the road, he heaved the tree into the back of the truck, put away the axe, and reached for his kindling and matches.

"Time to start the fire for our hot dogs. It will soon be lunchtime."

He put the tailgate down to use as a table. Jill set the cooler of goodies on it and got out the mugs.

"Too bad I didn't bring a plastic tablecloth," Jill lamented.

"Tablecloth? We're roughing it!" Dan laughed and finished preparing his fire. "See? I haven't quite forgotten how to start a fire."

Dan stepped back, folded his arms, and watched for the best time to put on the bigger pieces of wood he had brought.

The fire was soon blazing, sparks shooting up with a snap.

Jill opened the hot dog buns, put wieners on the sticks, and set out catsup and relish.

Dan picked up a stick with a hot dog and crouched in front of the fire. Jill did the same. She soon tottered in the crouch position, so she stood to hold her stick into the fire.

"You can laugh," she remarked as she watched him smile at her. "I didn't get to the Boy Scouts when I was young."

"I should hope not!" Dan chuckled. "Here, these are done. Want to sit on the tailgate?"

"Will it hold me?" Jill asked doubtfully.

"Would I ever offer you a seat that wouldn't hold you? I may chuckle sometimes, but I would never ask you to do something that might hurt you."

Jill kissed him. "I should never have doubted you."

She eased herself onto the tailgate after pouring coffee for them both.

"Hot dogs taste so much better outdoors than at a table." Dan took a bite loaded with catsup and relish. "I think even the coffee tastes better out here. Sure is good and hot."

"This is a great way to spend a winter morning." Jill took a bite of hot dog. It took a while to chew before she could add, "I'm so glad you thought of this."

"Me, too." Then, after a short pause, "Were you able to put in something for a sweet tooth?"

"Yup. Made these up last night." Jill produced some oatmeal and raisin cookies.

"My favorites. They look good."

Dan took a bite, wrinkled his nose, and looked at the cookie.

"What's wrong?" she asked. *What in the world did I miss?*

"Nice try—but I'm thinking there's too much baking soda. Do you remember what the recipe called for?"

"I think it was half a tablespoon."

"Well, maybe I've had to bake more than you did when you were going to school. I'd guess it was half a *teaspoon*—not a tablespoon."

Jill groaned. "Oh, dear. Guess I'd better look at those cookbooks more carefully. Honestly, Dan, preparing lessons for all these grades takes more time than I thought it would." She smiled at him ruefully. "I guess we'll give the birds a treat."

She flung the cookies into the snow.

"Not to worry," he said. "I'll survive without a cookie—this time. But I'm warning you about next time."

He laughed, pulled her close, and kissed her.

What a sweetheart. But I'll do better next time.

They sat a few more minutes in the peaceful quiet.

"Well, time to get this baby's feet in water." Dan patted the tree. "I think we made a good choice."

He helped Jill put things away, then closed the tailgate. When they were ready to go, they slid into the truck seat. They could see their breath in the cold cab.

"Guess I should have started this sooner to warm up," Dan apologized.

"It's not that far to the house. It will be warm there and we can have another cup of coffee to warm our insides."

Jill snuggled against Dan.

"I can hardly wait to see lights shining on my first Christmas tree," she said.

Dan hugged her shoulder before he started the motor.

Chapter 34

❧

"Isn't this great?" Jill leaned her head on Dan's shoulder. "What a difference it makes to have a lighted tree in the room."

"Yeah, I'm glad it worked out so well. I was a little afraid we were in trouble when we tipped the pail of water on the floor. Good thing the floor is linoleum!"

"There were lots of good things today," Jill added.

"When it gets dark this early, you have more time to enjoy the lights," Dan said.

Jill turned to look at him. "Are you getting ready for supper?"

"What do you have? I've noticed your fridge is never overly stocked. Never mind. You made breakfast. Let's go to town and I'll buy supper."

"I can't refuse an offer like that," Jill said. "But I'll admit that I'm feeling more and more at home here. I'll try to stock up my cupboard a little more." Jill got her coat and boots. "Since it's dark, I think I'll lock the door. Sometimes I'm a little nervous coming into the house at night after I've been gone."

"Of course you need to lock the door. Sometimes I can't believe how trusting you are."

"Except for Steve Webber—"

"Whoa, no shop talk," Dan said. "And don't let that man bother you."

"I try not to. But when I look at Melissa, something seems wrong."

"You don't have any proof. Just keep loving Melissa—which I know you do with all your kids."

Dan opened the door for Jill with a flourish.

"Christmas is coming. I'd better be good," he said with a chuckle. "Give me the key and I'll lock up."

The snow crunched under their boots as they walked to the truck. The stars were bright in the clear, dark sky.

"There's the Big Dipper," Jill pointed out, scanning the sky. "And Orion. I just wish I knew the names of more constellations." She jumped into the truck. "Brrrrr! Let's make sure to find a warm place to eat."

Dan groaned. "Think I'll ever learn to start the motor early?"

"If we can't stand fifteen minutes of a cold drive, we're not very hardy," Jill said, laughing. "We're prairie folk. We can manage a lot." She snuggled against Dan. "It's not as easy shifting gears with mitts on, is it?"

"No. But we're prairie folk. We can manage."

Dan grinned sideways at Jill as he pushed in the clutch for her to shift into second.

At the restaurant, they took a booth with an outside view. For a few minutes, they sat enjoying the city lights, but when they noticed the waiter about to approach, they hurriedly scanned their menus to make a choice.

Sipping their coffee, Jill asked, "Any ideas on what we should do with Joe and Marg during the holidays? I haven't forgotten that you told me to save New Year's Eve for a special dinner. Should we add them in?"

"Hey, you just told me this morning that she's coming. I haven't had time to think of Marg and Joe. I've only thought about you and the tree—and how hungry I'm getting." Joe glanced at his watch. "No wonder I'm hungry. It's six-thirty! Aren't you starved? Don't forget, we missed our cookies at lunch!"

"Whatever we decide will be fun," Jill said, ignoring him. "We had such a good time together at Thanksgiving. Say, looks like it's your lucky day. Here's supper. That should keep you from starving."

"Ahhh. Smells so good." Dan sniffed at his plate. "I'm really grateful for the good food here. Let's pray."

He reached over to hold Jill's hand while he prayed a blessing.

They lingered over the meal, talking about the coming holidays and plans.

"You know, the more the merrier," Dan said. "I'll ask Joe if he wants to bring Marg to the Bess on New Year's Eve. And as for some more ideas, I imagine Joe will want her to be with his family on Christmas Day. And I want to be with you Christmas Eve and Christmas Day."

"I'm looking forward to meeting your family, and having you meet mine," Jill agreed. "Christmas is time to be with family—and like you say, the more the merrier."

After the bill came, they headed to the parking lot.

At the house, Dan walked Jill to the door and unlocked it before kissing her goodnight.

"I'd better get back now. It's been a long day, but such a good one." He kissed her again. "Don't forget, I'll be here Thursday."

Jill flicked on her lights, locked the door, and listened as Dan drove away.

Chapter 35

Thursday morning came quickly. Jill walked through the freshly fallen snow on her sidewalk. As she stepped through the hedge, snow fell from the branches onto her shoulders. She mused at the placing of the hedge, but it did give her privacy from the road. Smoke was already drifting from the chimney, which meant Butch was inside making a fire.

At the school door, she took a deep breath.

This is a big day. Oh, I hope the program goes well tonight. Thank goodness Dan will be here to help. I wish Mom and Dad could come, but they won't tackle the snowy roads. At least I know I can count on Linda and Helen to help with getting the kids into their costumes and with the lunch afterwards. Thank You, Lord, for friends.

Opening the door, she greeted Butch.

"Thanks, Butch. You've already got the chill out of the room. I'm grateful you're so dependable."

Her commendation was met with a happy smile.

"You know, Miss Jackson," Butch said, "it actually gives me a good feeling to help. And the pay is nice, too."

"Well, you know the old verse: it really is more satisfying to be able to give than just to take. You've learned that early in life. Some people never learn it—they just keep taking."

"I'm kind of sorry for them, Miss Jackson. They turn into crabby, selfish old people. I know, because I've watched it happen to someone I know."

Jill waited, but Butch didn't go on and she didn't question him. Another puzzle added to her class collection.

Her thoughts turned to the parents. She hoped most of them would come. It would mean a lot to the students, who had worked so hard.

Jill sat at her desk and checked her lesson plans one more time. She planned to dismiss school at recess to give the children time to get home and back for the program.

Glancing at the clock, she saw that it was time to ring the bell. The class came in boisterously today, but she gave them a few minutes to hang up their wraps and sit down.

After *Oh Canada* and the Lord's Prayer, she informed them that they would do their reading and math in the morning, along with some printing or writing practice. "After lunch," she continued, "we'll go over the program one more time. I'll dismiss you at recess so you can be ready to come back in time for the program."

"How many of you know for sure that at least one of your folks will be here tonight?" she asked.

Every hand went up.

"We'll put all the desks off to the side so that we can have chairs for your folks to sit in the middle, where they can see," Jill said. "Now, let's start with reading. Ivan and Larry, you can read the next story in your reader. Grades Three and Four, I want you to do a comprehension exercise to make sure that you understand what you're reading. Sharon and Teresa, you can go to the back and take turns reading out loud to each other. Put expression into it. Mike and Butch, I want to sit with you and discuss the last story we did. Okay, you all know what to do for the next while. If you finish your work early, take out your library book until I can come help you."

Jill smiled at Mike and Butch as she pulled up a chair at their desks. "*Treasure Island* was written years ago. What did you think of Jim, the narrator? What was his life like at The Admiral Benbow? Did you think he was brave or foolish when he agreed to go to sea?"

Jill continued her questions for a while, then gave them an assignment. "Write about a time when you felt you had to do something hard. How did you feel? Were you able to accomplish it?"

Then she moved on to give time to Ivan and Larry. Larry had his usual grubby smell and his happy smile of greeting. She hugged his shoulder. Ivan's hair was slicked to his head and he wore a freshly ironed shirt.

Contrasts, contrasts, Jill thought as she brought her chair between their desks.

From the corner of her eye, she spied Mike looking at Butch's work. "Mike, you have something worth writing. I want *your* story," she admonished. Mike responded by folding his arms and slouching into his desk. "You're in Grade Seven. I'm sure that in your life you've had something hard or scary to do. Just tell it on paper like you would tell your friend what happened."

"Nothing scares me," he challenged.

"Okay, then just pretend. Or write about someone else who had to do something hard or scary."

Jill then turned her attention back to Ivan and Larry.

Butch got up to add wood to the fire.

Recess came and the children hurried outside for fresh air and a bathroom break, if they needed one. Marie rang the bell to call them back in for math. Over recess, Jill had printed a carol on the board for them to copy in their best handwriting.

The day was flying by. Noon brought the usual offers of trades from their lunch buckets and the smell of banana and orange peelings in the wastebasket.

Jill sat eating at her desk, watching her students.

Honey had on a lovely sweater and skirt. Across from her sat Melissa, who had red hair but no temper. Melissa smoothed her skirt while she ate her sandwich. It didn't appear that she had anything else in her bucket.

How that child appeals to me. What makes her so quiet? I'll watch for clues when her folks are here.

Dear Randy. He is such a helpful child. His mother was crippled some from polio, and Jill didn't know much about his dad, Sam, except that he was a postman as well as a farmer. But Randy, always slightly disheveled, was open and happy.

Sharon looked up from her lunch and smiled when she noticed Jill looking her way. *Always helpful, but never obtrusive,* Jill thought. *What a blessing it is to have her folks so close by.*

Teresa had removed her glasses while she ate her lunch. Mike ambled by and Teresa was just able to grab her glasses as Mike's hand brushed over her desk. Of course it was intentional. Mike just persisted in having a chip on his shoulder.

And Butch. Solid, polite Butch. It was a joy to have him in the class.

Jill looked at her watch. "Okay, let's clean up from lunch and go over our program."

She stood and got their illustrations ready for them to pick up when they did the recitation.

"First, I'll welcome your parents and guests," she said. "Then we'll start the program with everyone singing some carols. Mrs. Gilmore will lead us. I'll play the piano. Then Butch Taylor will read the Christmas story. Next, Marie will sing 'O Little Town of Bethlehem,' after which Sharon will play 'Joy to the World.' After that, we'll all come up and say our choral speech. Pick up your illustrations on the way to the front, and remember to hold the illustrations up high… and remember where you stand.

"Don't sit down after the choral speech. Mrs. Gilmore will lead us in another carol. Mrs. Martins will then help you put on your costumes and take your places. When you're all in your places for the Nativity, we'll sing 'Away in a Manger,' and then everyone will join in singing 'Silent Night.' After we finish singing, you can take off your costumes and hang them up.

"That will be the end of the program, and then we can enjoy some cookies and *rohalyki* while I visit with your folks. You may want to show them your scribblers and work."

The class went through their program just fine.

"If you do that well tonight, it will be great," Jill assured them. "Lay your illustrations and costumes in order."

The class took their seats.

"Let's put all the desks here in a row to leave room in the center for chairs. When you're done, pick up any scrap paper and get your coats. Don't forget to be here by ten minutes to seven, so we can start on time."

The class hurriedly scraped their chairs to the side, wadded some paper to put in the basket, then went for their coats and boots.

Mike couldn't seem to resist being a pest and giving Sharon's pigtail a yank. She returned the favor with an elbow in the midriff just as Jill caught them and called a truce. Jill was just in time, as Marie was already heading towards her with another tale to tell.

Jill went to the house and started peeling carrots for supper. It was a relief that Dan was bringing chicken and fries from Kentucky Fried Chicken. She set the table, adding a plate of pickles and a dish of butter.

It was nearly six when he turned up the driveway and hurried into the house.

"Let's eat while it's hot," he announced, putting the bag on the table. "I'm starved, smelling this stuff all the way out from Saskatoon."

They dove into the food.

"How was your day?" Jill asked.

"I'll tell you later. It could have been better." Dan just kept chewing on his chicken bone. "What about yours?"

"A good day. We had one practice before the kids dismissed. Now we'll just take what comes. It looks like all the parents will be here."

"I'd better go set up the chairs. Twenty should be enough, eh?"

"Sounds good. Linda and Helen will set up the coffee and juice and any goodies. Ivan is bringing a special Ukrainian treat."

When they were done eating, Jill stood up. "I'll get changed and meet you at the school ASAP."

She hurried to her bedroom while Dan got the key and started towards the school.

Jill peeked through her bedroom window and watched him stride along the path. She then got out her long wool skirt with the matching blue sweater. She combed her hair, tried to put the stubborn cowlick in place, applied some lipstick, and headed for the door.

Where did I put the key? I need to lock the door at night. Why can't I be more organized and put it in its place? Jill checked the usual places and finally found it just as she was getting anxious. She grabbed her coat and headed out.

Dan already had the chairs in place when she got to the school and both Linda and Helen were there getting the drinks ready.

"I have some carol sheets," Helen announced. "That way, you can pick some of your favorites and not just sing mine." Helen smiled and put the sheets where they would be handy.

The Orlicks and Kolisnyks were the first two families to arrive. Helen and Linda joined Jill in greeting them. "I'm glad you're not on an out-of-town run today," Jill said, shaking hands with Oscar Orlick.

The children sat in their desks as they arrived, and soon everyone was present and ready to begin.

Jill was delighted that the program went well. Parents sang carols, called out favorites, and clapped for the children. Now they were enjoying *rohalyki* and complimenting Olga Kolisnyk. Ihor patted his wife and his own rounded tummy and said, "Good cook." There was an air of camaraderie and good wishes.

Jill had no hint that before she left the school that night, she would learn Melissa's dreadful secret.

Chapter 36

∾

Jill enjoyed visiting with parents and matching them up with the students.

Joan Thompkins was a pleasant woman, but she looked a little harried. "How long have you lived here?" Jill enquired.

"About three years. We're almost homesteaders. Everything has to go into the farm to make it productive, so the house needs to wait. I'm a city girl, so I really miss having running water."

They paused as her husband joined them.

"This is Wes," Joan introduced. "He's the one with the farm background."

"Pleased to meet you," Wes commented.

"Do you do grain or mixed farming?" Jill asked. She knew enough about farming to know there was a difference.

"Both," Wes answered with a hint of deserved pride in his work. "We have purebred dairy cattle and wheat."

Jill wished them well and turned to some of the other parents.

"That was a lovely program," Ann Marie Wheeler said, coming up with her husband Ken. "It showed a lot of work. Thank you."

The Wheelers looked a little out of place in this farm community. Ann Marie had a newly coiffed hairdo and a beautifully-styled suit. Ken wore a gray three-piece suit, a white shirt, and a discreetly colored tie with a matching hankie tucked into his jacket pocket.

"I came straight from work," he said, explaining his business attire. "I guess you know I'm a bank manager, and it seems that the emergencies only come up when we want to leave early." He shrugged and gave a little laugh. "But I didn't want to miss the program. Honey has been talking about it all week."

"I'm glad you could come," Jill answered honestly.

"Well, thank you for your work here. Sorry we have to leave, but I have a purebred dog that gets a little high-strung when left home alone." Ken reached out to shake hands and wish Jill a merry Christmas.

Jill glanced around. *Bless Linda and Helen. I see that they're keeping the drinks and nibbles ready. Dan seems to be having a good time visiting, too.*

She turned as Mabel and Oscar Orlick approached.

"I hear you're a long-haul truck driver," Jill greeted. "I'm glad your schedule let you be here tonight."

"Yeah, I'm gone quite a bit," Oscar said. "I tell Mike to be a 'he-man' and look after things at home. Mabel keeps the home fires burning." Oscar turned and smiled at his wife.

Mabel said, "I grow a big garden and do lots of canning. Could I send a few jars with Mike tomorrow?"

"Why, that would be lovely," Jill said, smiling. "Thank you. I've never tried to can things. If I ever get time to can, I'll know who to call on for help."

"Hear that, Mike?" Mabel said. "You have a job tomorrow."

Mike didn't look happy at the prospect of bringing jars of food to his teacher.

"Aww, Ma, I have my hands full carrying my books."

"Books? What books?" Oscar said. "You're big enough to carry a few jars along with books." He turned to Jill. "Give us a call when you get them."

"I'll do that. And thank you again."

Jill wanted to speak to Andy Taylor, but Steve and Marcie Webber were approaching with Melissa.

"Good play." Steve strutted up with one thumb hooked into his suspenders and his arm around Melissa's shoulder. Marcie Webber stood behind. She was short and pale in complexion. Her dress was obviously homemade.

Jill immediately felt sorry for her. Marcie seemed ill at ease as she smoothed her dress and brushed her hair back.

Jill turned her attention to Steve. "I'm glad you and your wife could come."

"I thought Melissa would play an angel," Steve went on.

"She could have," Jill answered, "but we needed someone special for Mary. I thought she did a beautiful job as Mary."

Steve persisted. "That's true, but somehow to me Melissa is always an angel. She's my special angel—aren't you, Melissa?"

Melissa was looking at the floor. The color had drained from her cheeks. She stood brushing her skirt.

"Aren't you, Melissa? My special angel—pure as new snow."

While Melissa turned to say, "Yes, Papa," Jill's mind whirled. *Steve's possessive hold on Melissa… Marcie standing behind… Steve's insistence on calling Melissa "my special angel" and Melissa's obvious discomfort. The day she got sick so suddenly when the kids were going out to play snow angel… I've wondered all year what makes Melissa so withdrawn at times. Could it be? Surely not. Could Steve be using Melissa as his sex angel?*

Jill felt suddenly ill. She knew her face showed her revulsion. She had never been able to mask her feelings. She clenched her fists and forced a reply, but she hadn't recovered quickly enough. Steve's color had become a deep red and the veins at the side of his neck bulged.

Realizing that he suspected her misgivings, she concluded with fear that her neighbor from two miles down the road was her enemy as well as Melissa's. She turned to Marcie, who was looking at the floor.

"Thank you both for coming," Jill managed.

"Good night," Steve said coldly. "We need to get going." He gripped Melissa's shoulder and turned abruptly. "Get your coat, Marcie."

Marcie gave a quick, embarrassed "Goodnight" to Jill, then turned to grab her coat.

Steve marched toward the door, his boots clomping on the floor. Without waiting for Marcie, he slammed the door shut behind him. Marcie fluttered behind, a wounded sparrow who couldn't fly.

Jill forced herself to greet the remaining parents and to thank Linda and Helen for their help.

Finally, the last people left.

"What in the world is wrong?" Dan asked, coming up and putting his arms around her. "Everything went so well."

"Oh, Dan, I've heard of parents abusing their children. It's so revolting. But something happened tonight, and now I think I know why Melissa is so withdrawn sometimes. So quiet."

She repeated her conversation with Steve Webber.

"What a terrible man," she said. "How could he do such a thing?"

She leaned against Dan for support.

He hugged her and stroked her hair. "It looks possible, but you have no real proof—"

"But it all fits," Jill interrupted. "Melissa's sudden illness at the thought of playing snow angel… Steve's insistence that Melissa should have been an angel in the Nativity… the way all his focus was on Melissa and not on his wife… oh Steve. I hope I'm wrong."

It's just that I've wondered so long about Melissa's periods of withdrawal. This would explain it. Horribly.

"Yes, it looks that way, but I'm concerned about you, Jill. As hard as it is to admit, you don't have firm proof yet. Keep loving Melissa. Keep encouraging her. But don't," he took Jill's shoulders and looked her in the eye, "don't let yourself hate Steve."

"How can I help it?"

"Only through prayer, I'd say. Jill, I saw hatred take over my father's life and relationships. I can't bear to think of hatred taking hold in your life. It will spread like a weed and affect all your other relationships." He kissed her. "Now, let me put the chairs away. The kids can straighten the desks in the morning. We need to get out of here."

Jill nodded and put some notes together while Dan put away the chairs.

Dear Dan. What a support he is. I know he's right about not hating Steve, but what an awful bully… his own daughter. Jill shuddered at the thought of Steve with little Melissa.

"Ready?" Dan asked. He had stored the chairs while she pondered the situation.

"You bet. Thanks so much. What would I do without you?" she breathed.

They locked the doors and walked to the west end of the teacherage to let themselves in.

"Is there time for hot chocolate?" she asked. "I didn't have a drink at the program. Did you try the *rohalyki*? I slipped a couple of extra pieces into my purse."

Dan grinned. "Good plan."

Jill put on the kettle and got the hot chocolate ready. When the water was hot, she poured and stirred, then added some cream from the fridge.

Dan was already sitting on the couch with the tree lights on when she came in with their hot chocolate and *rohalyki.*

"This is so good," he said. "You, Christmas lights, hot chocolate, and *rohal*—however you say it."

Jill snuggled against him. "And tomorrow afternoon starts the Christmas holidays. Are you able to pick me up after school? I'll need to get to the bank to cash my check."

"Is there snow in the Arctic? Of course I'll pick you up." He squeezed her shoulder, pulling her closer. "It's my pleasure."

After a few minutes, Dan checked the time. "Gracious, it's after eleven and we both have to work tomorrow."

Dan stretched, got up, and prepared to leave. Jill followed him to the door and kissed him ardently.

Sometimes it's so hard to see him leave.

He gave her one extra hug.

"Don't forget," he warned. "Don't let hatred for Steve take hold."

I'll do my best, she vowed as she heard Dan drive away.

Jill turned the key in the lock, checked the blinds, and turned off the kitchen light. The exchange with Steve had left her a little uneasy. It would be good to get away for the holidays.

Chapter 37

∾

After recess on Friday, Jill let the kids choose their favorite Christmas songs to sing. Then she passed out the Christmas cookies she had made. While the students munched, she let them share their Christmas holiday plans. Everyone was getting excited. Christmas was definitely in the air.

Mike was to go on a long-haul trip with his dad. Ivan's grandmother was coming for a weeklong visit. Teresa was traveling on the bus alone to Medicine Hat after Christmas to see her grandma and visit a cousin. Only Melissa and Butch had no plans to share.

"Well, let's clean up and get ready," Jill announced. "Butch, you can leave the sweeping tonight. Just check the stove. You can get a key from Mrs. Martins if you want to come in during the holiday. I'll be in Saskatoon. Have a special holiday. I'll see you Tuesday morning, January 3."

Jill helped Larry zip up his jacket. Randy noticed that Ivan was having trouble getting his boots on, so he hurried over to help. Sharon gathered the brushes for a quick swat, so they would be ready when school resumed.

"Miss Jackson, thank you for all you do for us," Butch said.

Jill turned to see Butch standing with his cap in his hand.

"Butch, you are so welcome. And thank you for all you do here. I hope you and your dad have a good Christmas together. I'm sure there are times when holidays are hard without your mom."

Butch nodded solemnly and turned to leave.

I'm not taking any work home for the holidays, so before I leave I'd better plan something for the first day back.

Jill sat down at her desk. She took a few moments to think back over the past four months, then resolutely picked up her pen and plan book. After half an hour, she returned to her house. Her suitcase was packed. She checked again for her paycheck.

What a mess it would be if I showed up at the bank without my check! I'll have to ration this one to last until the end of January, but it will be fun to have some extra moolah for the holiday.

Dan's truck turned into the driveway as she daydreamed.

"Ready?" Dan was at the door.

Jill nodded and reached for her purse.

Dan picked up her suitcase. "What's in here? Bricks?"

"Clothes and stuff," Jill answered vaguely. *Dan's gift is heaviest. Oh, I hope he likes it.*

"Are your folks expecting you for supper?" he asked. "Or can we have a bite when you're finished at the bank?"

"It's funny. After four months on my own, it seems strange to be going home for Christmas holidays. I only told them I'd be home tonight—no particular time. Supper would be fun, a celebration of the week off."

"When's Marg coming?"

"She's staying in Rosthern for Christmas and coming down Boxing Day Monday until New Year's afternoon. It will be fun having her."

"Joe's sure happy she's coming. He's even tidied up his apartment to make a good impression. Usually it's a mess," he added with a friendly grin. "Be careful. He's planning to make dinner for the four of us. It will be fun, but he hasn't got a reputation yet as a gourmet cook."

"I don't think I've earned my gourmet cook reputation, either," Jill said, ruefully remembering her bad batch of cookies. "Well, I did practice making a pumpkin pie, so I'll try not to have a disaster for you when you come for Christmas dinner. I made one and took it to the Martins one night. They didn't complain, so I guess it wasn't too bad."

"They'd better not complain. Did I complain about the cookies? No. Did the birds enjoy finding them? I'll bet they did—and I'll check the cook's lips to see if the pie is edible."

The bank was open late Friday. Jill counted her money and stashed it in her purse, feeling quite satisfied. At the restaurant, Dan put her suitcase in the cab before locking the door.

Supper was cozy with Christmas music and everyone cheerful. Dan arranged to pick up Jill for Christmas Eve dinner at his folks. Then they'd go to a candlelight service at church. Jill said she was sure Christmas Day turkey dinner would be at six o'clock, but she would check with her mom.

It was so pleasant sitting across the table from Dan and making plans. She almost hated to go home, but she knew her folks were waiting.

"Guess I'd better make tracks," she said a little reluctantly. "I drew Joanne's name for Christmas this year, and I still need to buy her a present. Since it's my first Christmas with a paycheck, I bought something special for my folks—some Guy Lombardo records. I still need to wrap them." Jill let out a laugh. "Don't worry. Yours will be ready for tomorrow night. Actually, I'm the one who's worrying. I sure hope you like the gift I chose. Well, time will tell—I won't!"

"I'll like it because you chose it," Dan assured her.

They headed into a night sparkling with Christmas lights and falling snow.

"You know, I really don't know where your folks live in Saskatoon," Dan said. "You'll have to direct me."

"Sure. You know where City Hospital is? Well, we live just north of there on Seventh Avenue. Near the drugstore."

When they pulled up to the house, Dan carried her suitcase to the door.

"See you tomorrow at about four o'clock," he said, then kissed her and left her at the door.

Chapter 38

∾

"Hi everyone," Jill announced as she opened the unlocked front door.

"You're a little late," Joanne said by way of greeting.

"I didn't know there was a set time to arrive," Jill muttered.

Wow. What a welcome. What a way to start my week here.

Before she could think of an answer for Joanne, her folks came around the corner.

"Hello, little girl," her father said, hugging her affectionately.

"Oh, Dad. It's so good to see you."

Jill hugged her dad and then stepped back to look at him. His gray hair was thinning. *Why didn't I notice sooner how stooped he's getting?* She hugged him again.

"My turn," her mom announced.

"Merry Christmas, Mom. The kitchen smells good already. What are you baking?"

"Well," her mom started, "I baked a chicken for your welcome supper. That's probably what you smell."

"Told you that you're late," added Joanne accusingly.

"Mom, you never told me to be here by supper. I'm sorry," Jill finished lamely.

"Don't worry, Jill. The rest of us enjoyed a good dinner. Have you eaten? There's leftovers."

Dear Dad. Always the peacemaker. Always ready to pour oil on troubled water. What would this family do without him?

"Yes, Dad, I had a bite—enough to last until breakfast. But thanks for offering. The chicken does smell good."

Jill picked up her suitcase and carried it to her old room. Everything looked the same, but it somehow felt different coming back for a week after having her own place for four months. Besides, Dan was in her life now, and that made everything different.

Jill opened her suitcase and began hanging up her clothes.

Soon Joanne was at the door, eyeing her critically.

"Staying in here all night?" Joanne asked. "Mom and Dad would like a visit, you know. You haven't been here for months."

"It's a little hard to walk fifteen miles—or maybe you didn't know I don't have a car," Jill answered coldly.

"You don't need to be snide."

Jill turned, but Joanne had walked off, preventing a reply.

Lord, how will I stand a whole week of this? Why can't we be friends?

Jill finished unpacking, combed her hair, and reached for a box of chocolates she had brought.

She went out to the living room and found her folks each sitting in their favorite chair. Joanne had disappeared. Opening the box, Jill offered them each a chocolate.

"Sweets for the sweet," she chirped.

They each took one. Jill left the opened box on the table beside her mom.

"So, any special plans for the next week?" she asked. "And what time is Christmas dinner? I told Dan I thought it was at six."

"It's always been six, so I guess we won't change now," her mom answered. "But if Dan wants to come early, we'd love to meet him."

"I'll ask," Jill promised. "By the way, would it be okay if I make a pumpkin pie for dessert?"

She tried to make it sound offhand, but it came out a little stiff. Jill had never offered to make dessert before.

"I'd be glad for the help," her mom said. "If you don't make pie, we'll just have ice cream and cookies."

They settled back in their chairs to chat. Her folks brought her up to date on neighbors. Mrs. Brewer had been ill. Her friend, Mrs. Curtiss, had helped her with some cleaning and cooking. Jill told them that she intended to visit Mrs. Brewer and ask about her years of teaching experience.

They talked about the events of the past few months, and about their health. Jill was concerned when she learned that her dad was being treated for a mini-stroke he'd had in November.

Her folks asked about school, the students, the Christmas program, and how she liked living in the teacherage. Jill told them of the fun she'd had looking for a tree and decorating it.

"This Dan sounds like a nice guy. I'm eager to check him out," her dad commented. "You know, a dad can be quite protective when a guy comes courting his daughter."

Jill smiled. "I think he'll pass, but I'll listen to your opinion."

They talked about some of the plans for the week.

"When Marg comes, she can share my room," Jill suggested. "That way, it won't make extra laundry for you, Mom."

"I remember Marg being here when you were both in Teacher's College. She's a pleasant girl."

"Pleasant, yes, but she needs a few more pounds under that curly head of hair," Dad added.

"I still need to get Joanne's present. Has she dropped any hints about what she wants?"

"The only thing that interests that girl is clothes," her dad responded.

"Now, Tom, that isn't entirely true. She likes to look good in public. I guess I can take the blame for that," Mom said, looking at her husband in his comfortable cardigan and slippers. "But she's interested in joining my swim club. I've seen her reading *Readers Digest*. Maybe she'd like a subscription."

Jill reviewed the brief possibilities and decided to take a trip downtown in the morning. She could enjoy the Christmas decorations and hopefully find something Joanne would like. She considered asking her mom if she wanted to come along, but then decided against it. She'd just make a quick trip.

Her mom's voice soon interrupted her thoughts. "Why don't I come with you? We could have a nice mother-daughter lunch. Maybe Joanne could join us. She gets half an hour for lunch and they have a cafeteria at the store."

Mom looked expectantly at Jill.

"Sure, Mom. That would be fine if you came, but it would be nice to find a quiet restaurant for lunch instead of gobbling our food in half an hour, part of which would be spent standing in line to pick it up."

Her mom looked a little crestfallen, but Jill assured her that a quiet lunch would be better than a rushed one and pointed out that she could meet Joanne when the stores were less crowded.

During the discussion, her dad quietly stretched his legs, bent his toes back and forth, and studied the pictures on the wall.

"Jill, I want you to know how proud we are of you," he said. "It sounds a little like you have a special man in your life, but I'm your first special man, and I'd like to take you to lunch myself once this week. How does that sound?"

"Dad, I'd love it. Let's go Monday before Marg gets here."

Jill relished the thought. Time just to sit with her Dad. To chat. To ask him things she wished she'd asked before about his early life. Her mind started filling up with things she wanted to know.

She smiled at him and patted his hand, assuring him that, indeed, he was her first special man.

Looking a little petulant, her mom added, "Well, I'll just have to settle for lunch tomorrow."

"One special lunch each," Jill soothed. "Want another chocolate?"

"I'd better pass. I need to watch my weight." Her mom watched her husband, who picked one out happily.

"Thanks," he said. "I haven't had a chocolate for a long time. This one's nice and soft."

Jill set the box on the table and checked her watch. "If you don't mind, I'll go to bed now. Morning will be here soon and we have a big day."

After giving each of them a goodnight kiss on their cheeks, she headed to her room, already looking forward to Christmas Eve at Dan's.

Chapter 39

Jill woke and stretched. She could smell toast and coffee. The sun wasn't up yet, but she enjoyed thinking about the fact that the days were getting longer now. It would just be a little longer before she woke to sunlight.

Hearing her mother puttering in the kitchen noisily, she knew it was time to get up. Today was Christmas Eve. She'd go shopping this morning with her mom and, this evening, she would meet Dan's mother and father. The thought was both exciting and scary. It was exciting to be part of their family Christmas Eve. It was scary thinking how important this meeting would be. Would she make a good impression?

"Jill, breakfast is ready."

"I'll be out in a jiffy, Mom."

She hurried out of bed, splashed some water on her face, yanked a comb through her hair, and pulled on the clothes she had worn yesterday.

There. It'll have to do.

She strolled into the kitchen.

"Good morning, everyone," she said as she poured herself a coffee. She kissed her Dad's balding head as she sat down.

"One for me, too?"

"Of course," Jill mumbled, getting up to give her mom a peck on the cheek. "It's great to wake up to the smell of fresh coffee. Thanks."

"What time do you think we'll be back from town?" her mom asked. "I have a hair appointment at two-thirty. Do you want me to check if you can come in, too?"

"No thanks, Mom. I don't want to take time to sit in the salon today. Don't worry," she added, "I won't embarrass you. I'll fix my hair."

Her mother sniffed slightly, indicating she was a little offended, but she said nothing.

"Let's try to leave by ten," Jill said. "That'll give us time for a little shopping and a leisurely lunch. We'll easily be back before your appointment. Then Dad and I can have an afternoon coffee before Dan picks me up."

Joanne came in to join them. With a cursory "Good morning," she poured herself a coffee and sat down.

"Did I hear you say Dan is picking you up today?" Joanne asked. "What about our Christmas Eve? When will we open our gifts?"

"I told Mom that I'm spending Christmas Eve with Dan. He's joining us tomorrow for Christmas Day dinner. We can open our gifts tomorrow morning, or you can open them tonight and I'll open mine in the morning. You can go ahead with the usual Christmas Eve without me."

"Typical. You plan your life and we'll adjust."

Jill almost experienced the old adage to "bite your tongue." She avoided a reply.

Dad stirred his coffee noisily before slurping it. That broke the exchange. He never slurped his coffee. Joanne recognized that it was a signal for her to be quiet.

"It's good to have you here at the table again," her dad acknowledged. "You have a good day and I'll look forward to coffee this afternoon."

Jill smiled gratefully at her Dad. *What a treasure he is. What a wise peacemaker.*

Their breakfast was soon over. Joanne left for work and Jill cleared the table.

"I'll be ready at ten, Mom. I guess we'll take the bus, eh?"

"It will likely be easier than finding a place to park today," Mom replied before leaving the kitchen to get dressed for town.

Jill poured more coffee for herself and Dad.

"There's no rush," she said. "I'll just enjoy sitting with you a little longer. Somehow it seems so normal to be at the breakfast table, yet it's been four months since you helped me move to Brentville. After all this time, I'm still enjoying teaching. Some problems, some achievements. I guess that's life."

"Yes, Jill. If everything in our life was our achievements, we'd tend to become complacent and self-satisfied. The problems, while we don't enjoy them, make us realize that we need help, and they can make us turn to God. Unfortunately, problems make some people bitter and they turn away from the help they need."

Jill enjoyed just sitting and sharing with her dad. She hadn't realized how much she missed times like these. But glancing at her watch, she excused herself to get ready for town.

At ten o'clock, she and her mom were ready to catch the next bus.

It was an uneventful morning. Jill found a nice scarf for Joanne in her favorite colors, then she and her mom had a leisurely lunch. Jill was happy to pick up the tab.

Mom is picky, but she's not confident in herself. I wonder where she got to feeling so conscious of everyone else's opinions? She's well-liked. A good cook. She's active in her swim club. Dad loves her. Ah, it's a mystery that I'm not going to solve.

They gathered their coats and headed for the bus stop.

It was only one-thirty when they stepped in the door. Jill headed to her room to wrap Joanne's gift so that it would be ready if they opened gifts tonight. She had already wrapped the record for her folks. Dan's gift was wrapped, too. She took it from her suitcase and set it out with the other gifts. It had taken so much thought in choosing, but she wasn't sure even now if it was "right."

"I'm leaving," she heard her mother announce. "I should be back by four-thirty."

Jill went to the door. "You'll come back looking great. Dan is picking me up at four o'clock, so I'll wish you a lovely Christmas Eve and see you in the morning."

When her mom left, she turned to her dad.

"One more cup of coffee?" she asked.

"Wouldn't miss it." He smiled and headed to the kitchen table.

They visited, reminisced about some favorite holidays, and talked a little about Dan.

"I'm glad he's welcome here tomorrow," Jill said. "You'll get to meet him and give me your opinion. I really want to know what you think." She stood after a while. "Well, I guess I'd better get ready. I want to look okay when he introduces me to his folks."

Dad smiled and patted her hand. "If they don't think you look okay, they need glasses."

He chuckled and watched her go to her room.

Chapter 40

❦

J ill checked herself in the mirror and went to the living room. She put the gifts for her folks and Joanne by the fireplace, where they would be found if the family followed the tradition of opening them on Christmas Eve. Her father had left the room.

She sat down to wait for Dan. Her tummy was a little tight. This was going to be a big night! Would this be the night she got a ring? Maybe he would propose tonight.

Jill had long ago learned to recognize the sound of Dan's truck. When she heard him drive up, she rose to meet him at the door carrying her gifts for Dan and his parents.

"Scared?" he asked with a smile. "Well, don't be. My folks are just ordinary people—like me."

What a guy. Sounds like he's a mind-reader right now.

"Not scared," she replied. "A little nervous, I guess. It's such a special time, Christmas Eve, and the first time meeting your folks…"

"I guarantee they won't bite," Dan said, chuckling. "And my guess is they'll fall for you just like I have."

Dan opened the truck door and helped her in.

"Two gifts?" he asked, looking at her lap.

"Well, I wrapped my hostess gift. It's chocolates. That seemed safe, since I don't know your folks yet."

"A hostess gift? I never thought of that for your folks tomorrow."

"Not to worry. We've had lots of company through the years who came without a gift."

"Looks like you won't be helping shift gears lugging those two presents. Guess I'll have to do my own shifting—worse luck."

They drove in silence across the river and then turned into an area with large homes set back from the street. Most of the landscaped yards featured beautiful old trees. Christmas lights glowed in the windows.

They pulled up to the curb and Dan announced, "This is it." He jumped out to open Jill's door.

Jill was impressed. The house looked lovely—the stone chimney with the smoke curling up, the stone flower planters, and the tall evergreens near the door.

Dan's mother welcomed them at the door as Dan introduced Jill. Val Fischer was a warm, hospitable woman and Jill liked her immediately.

"Sit by the Christmas fire and be comfortable," Dan's mom said. "Would you like a cup of tea?"

"I'd love to sit by the fire, but I think I'll pass on the tea. Thanks anyway." Jill set her gift for Dan at the coat rack, took off her snowy boots, and pulled on some slippers before passing the hostess gift to Dan's mother.

"What's this?" Valerie exclaimed.

"Just a little thank you for having me to this special dinner," Jill explained.

"How thoughtful. We're glad to have you. Dan hasn't said much, but we knew he was spending a lot of time somewhere." Val smiled at her son.

They sat down and had a pleasant time getting acquainted. Val brought Dan up to date on the latest news gathered at the hair salon. He made a few offhand comments, then talked about all the extra hours at work doing Christmas accounts.

Finally, Dan's father, Willis, came in. He had a pronounced limp and his color was pale. Jill thought he didn't look well.

Dan introduced her and Willis came to shake her hand before sitting down stiffly in a straight-backed chair.

"So, I hear you're a teacher," Willis began abruptly.

"Yes, Mr. Fischer," Jill said. "That was my dream when I was still a girl. I feel fortunate to have a school close to Saskatoon."

"Makes it handy for Dan," Willis commented.

There was a moment of silence when Dan interjected, "How are you feeling, Dad? Is the weather affecting your arthritis?"

"Always does, you know," was the rather terse reply.

Jill felt a little uncomfortable.

Val asked her husband if he wanted some hot tea or coffee, but he declined.

"Will you be going with us to the Christmas Eve service, Dad?"

"Nope. Too hard to sit on those pews. I'll just stay here and likely go to bed early. I'm not up to those midnight services anymore."

"How about you, Mom? Will you come with us?" Dan continued evenly.

"I'd be a fifth-wheel," she answered, a little disappointed.

"Nonsense," Jill interrupted. "The Christmas Eve service is to be shared. We'd love to have you come with us—wouldn't we, Dan?" She looked at Dan.

He beamed. "That's right, Mom. You'll love the service. We'll need to leave by ten-thirty to find a place to park. It starts at eleven, doesn't it?"

"Well, if you're sure, I'd love to come," Val said. "Yes, the service starts at eleven. There will be an organ prelude starting at about ten-forty-five."

"Then we'll leave at ten-fifteen," Dan said. "The church isn't far. I know Jill will want to hear the prelude, too." He paused. "Will we still have pie and ice cream after the service?"

"You bet," his mom said. "Some traditions need to be kept alive."

Val headed to the kitchen to check on the ham. Jill followed her and offered to help set the table and prepare vegetables. They were soon chatting happily in the kitchen while they worked.

"That ham smells so good," Jill told her. "I haven't done much cooking. This is my first time on my own and my first year teaching. Usually dinner plans take a back seat to lesson plans."

Jill chuckled as she continued setting the table, folding Christmas napkins for each place, finding the salt and pepper shakers and the pitcher of ginger ale fruit punch.

It was so easy talking to Val and working with her. Jill couldn't help thinking of her own mom. She loved her mom, and she knew her mom loved her, but somehow they were often so careful with each other.

I wonder why Mom and I can't be relaxed like this. If I marry Dan, will it always be this way with Val? And what about Willis? He's the stiff one here. My dad is so warm and easy to talk to.

"Would you mind mashing the sweet potatoes?" Val called into the living room.

Dan sauntered in and took the masher. "I'll mash them to a pulp," he threatened. "Do they have salt and pepper? Butter? A little nutmeg?"

Val laughed. "Yes, yes. Just mash."

Val sliced the ham and arranged the slices on a platter. She gave Jill the salad to put on the table along with pickles, fresh buns, butter, and applesauce for the ham.

Dan finished mashing the sweet potatoes and put them in a bowl. Then he opened the oven and took out the roasted vegetables.

When everything was on the table, Val called Willis. Dan dimmed the dining room chandelier and lit the candles in the centerpiece.

They took their seats and Dan held Jill's hand as Val prayed a blessing on the food and on their time together. It was all so pleasant—except for Willis, who seemed determined not to participate much in the conversation. Jill noticed that Dan and his mom went ahead talking without trying to coax Willis to join.

The conversation was smooth with occasional light laughter. They talked about favorite holidays, about personal escapades at school. Dan shared a joke he had heard at the office and Jill recounted their tree hunting expedition, right down to the cookie failure.

When dinner was over, Val passed around Christmas mints. "No dessert until we get home," she said, smiling. "As soon as we've cleared the table, let's go sit around the fire and put on some Christmas music."

Dan and Jill cleared the table while Val put things away in the kitchen.

"I'll wash," offered Dan, and Jill offered to dry the dishes.

"That's great. Then I can put them away. There's never enough counter space in a kitchen," Val confided to Jill. "I'm convinced they only use men to design kitchens. I could give them some good ideas if they'd let me. But fat chance of that."

Val shrugged her shoulders and grinned.

Once the dishes were all put away, they headed for the living room. Willis was waiting in his chair with his feet up on a footstool. Dan put on some Christmas music and stirred the fire.

"Don't build it up too much," Willis ordered. "It'll need to die down when you three leave for the service. We don't want a house fire."

Jill knew by Dan's tight grip on the poker that he was annoyed at his father, but he said nothing as he added some wood and closed the screen. The record changed from "Joy to the World" to Handel's "Messiah."

"This music always gives me goose bumps," Jill commented when it got to the Hallelujah chorus. "No wonder people stand when it's played in a public setting."

"Stand if you want," Willis said.

"I think I'll pass here. Somehow a house doesn't seem to qualify as a public performance," Jill defended, a little embarrassed.

"Quite a bit of snow this year," Dan broke in. "Should be good for the farmers come spring."

"Yes, if we don't get too much wind and blow it away."

Dan's father is a real pessimist. I wonder, was he always like this?

After hearing the record to the end, Dan suggested it was time to get ready to leave.

"I'll just say goodnight and get ready for bed." Dan's father gripped the arms of the chair and slowly got to his feet. He gave Jill a nod. "Good to meet you."

"Yes, thank you. And a happy Christmas to you," she added.

Dan, Jill, and Val soon made their way to Dan's truck for the drive to the church.

Chapter 41

"What a lovely service," Jill exclaimed when they were on their way back. "That organist is terrific. Almost made the rafters shake sometimes."

In a few moments, they were back at the house.

"Pie and ice cream coming up," Val announced. "Does anyone want tea or coffee?"

"I'll have hot chocolate if you have any," Dan said. "How about you, Jill?"

"Tea sounds fine to me."

Val bustled around the kitchen cutting pie and putting it on plates. Dan dished up the ice cream. Jill made the tea and a cup of hot chocolate.

As soon as they were finished eating their pie, Val got up.

"I'm so glad you were here tonight, Jill. I really enjoyed sharing the evening with you and Dan," she said sincerely. "But I'm heading to bed. Have a merry Christmas."

I'll soon know what Dan has in mind. Keep cool, Jill. Don't let your anticipation show. And how I hope he likes what I got for him.

"Time to open our gifts, wouldn't you say? Then I'd better get you home before your folks call out a search warrant." Dan smiled at Jill, which made her heart jump.

Jill produced the heavy gift for Dan. "Mine first then."

"So this is the 'brick' that was in your suitcase? I'm not up to guessing, but I can tell it isn't a shirt!"

Dan pulled the wrapping off and lifted the lid. He held the tie up and admired it.

"Just the right color for my suit. And a matching hankie. Looks like you have good taste in men's apparel." He chuckled. "Now I'd better get out the brick!"

Jill watched as he lifted out a top quality hatchet and hammer. His eyes sparkled as he thanked her. "You must have noticed how worn my old hatchet was getting. This one is a beauty." He held it up, checked the blade, and admired it. "These will be a permanent addition to my toolbox on the truck."

Dan set them aside carefully in the box.

"Now I have something for you that I hope you'll like. I didn't realize how hard it is to find a gift for a girl."

Jill laughed. "Try shopping for a guy. Now that's what I call hard!"

Jill tried not to look too excited when Dan brought out a small box beautifully wrapped.

"I had the clerk wrap it," he commented. "I'm not up to this fussy stuff. I'm better wielding a hatchet."

Almost shyly, he presented the box to Jill.

Her heart pounded as she carefully removed the ribbon and paper. Lifting the lid, she pulled aside the tissue and found—not a ring, but—a beautiful locket.

Swallowing her disappointment, she lifted it out to admire it. "It's so dainty," she managed to say. "Thank you. I'll be proud wearing it."

"You can open it—put a picture inside," Dan advised. He moved close and gently opened the locket. It contained small pictures of Jill and himself.

"I don't remember you taking these!" Jill exclaimed. "What a special keepsake."

Dan took the locket and fastened it around Jill's neck. "Now you won't forget me." He kissed her slowly. "Merry Christmas, my darling."

Jill responded happily.

"Now it's time to get you home," he said.

Dan reached for their coats. Jill pulled her snow boots on and headed with Dan to the truck.

"Well, I told you they wouldn't bite, didn't I? You and Mom hit it off great." Dan put his arm around her shoulder. "What did you think of Dad?"

"To tell the truth, I'm not sure. He doesn't look well—his color, I mean. He seems more gruff than I expected, seeing as you're his son and not at all gruff."

"I wish you could have met Dad earlier. He was fun. Always talking to us. The change came when my grandfather died. For some reason, he left almost everything to Dad's brother. It's terrible to make a difference like that in the way you treat your kids. Dad never got over it. First he thought his brother would share. When that didn't happen, he got angry at both his father and his brother. That poisoned family gatherings. The hatred took root and spread, and now it affects his whole life—including Mom and me." Dan sighed. "I'm afraid this is the only Willis you will see."

"That's all so sad," Jill responded.

"Tragic, you might say."

They drove on in silence.

All too soon, they were back at her parents' place. The Christmas lights were off at most homes along the way.

Christmas lights off and my Christmas hope hanging.

Dan saw her to the door. After one more slow kiss, he said, "Good night. See you tomorrow."

Dan waited until he saw she was safely in the house before starting the motor and driving away.

Jill slowly made her way through the darkened house to her old room.

I know I love that guy, and I'm sure he loves me. So, what's the holdup? What's he waiting for? We've exchanged gifts, so there won't be any ring this Christmas. Well, I can still just enjoy the week with him. I love being with him, but if we get married, it will be because he wants it, too. As much as I want it.

Chapter 42

∾

Jill slept in and woke to the comforting smell of fresh coffee.

Christmas morning, back in my own bed in the family home. It feels so good, yet so different coming back after having my own place.

Jill stretched each muscle and then headed for the shower. She'd need to hurry. She could hear her mother bustling around the kitchen. It didn't take long before she was dressed.

"Good morning. Merry Christmas," she gushed.

Joanne and her folks were waiting.

"Took you long enough," Joanne griped.

"Sorry. The bed felt good and I slept in."

Dad, the peacemaker, remarked, "Well, she's here now. Merry Christmas to you, too."

Jill poured coffee and sat down. "How was your Christmas Eve service?"

"The usual," Joanne replied.

"Very nice," her dad commented. "And yours?"

"Excellent. Beautiful organ music, great worship time."

"What did you get from Dan for Christmas?" Joanne asked, barely concealing her curiosity.

"A beautiful locket with our pictures in it."

"No ring?"

"I've only known him four months. No, no ring. Do you really think I wouldn't have told you if we were engaged?"

Don't get upset, Jill. She's likely jealous. Don't let her spoil this special morning. Keep calm.

"By the way, Mom, I think I have all the ingredients with me for the pumpkin pie. Will you help me with the crust? I don't have your years of experience and I want it to be nice for Christmas dinner."

"I'd love to help. It's nice to see your interest in cooking. I must admit, I'm a pretty good cook—if I say so myself."

"Mom, you're the best cook I know. I'll be learning from a pro." Jill's compliment was sincere and her mother basked in it.

Breakfast was soon over. Jill gathered her materials for the pie while her dad went into the living room and lit the fire in the fireplace.

"A fire is such a pleasant way to take the chill off," he explained.

"I love a crackling fire," Jill agreed. Her mind went back to her first campfire with Dan.

Soon she and her mom were working on the pie crust. They turned on the oven, then set to work. Jill had a recipe for the filling, which looked big enough for two pies. They decided to put half in the fridge for a future pie or a pumpkin pudding.

The oven beeped when it was warmed up.

They poured in the filling. Jill carefully fluted the edge of the crust and put the pie in the oven.

"Want another cup of coffee?" Jill asked her mom once she had set the timer. "There's more in the pot."

As Jill sat with her mother, she felt a kitchen camaraderie she hadn't felt before. It was an intimate feeling.

"Where's Joanne?" she wondered aloud.

"Gone to a friend's for lunch."

"Anyone special?

"Just Rosie. They've been friends for years. Oh, and I almost forgot, thanks for the record. Dad has already been playing it. And I'll get your gift. Dad had your name."

"I've got it right here," Dad announced, coming into the kitchen. "I'll make the official Christmas presentation."

He smiled, then leaned over Jill to kiss her forehead and lay the gift in her lap.

"I think this is something that interests you," Dad commented as Jill tore off the wrapping paper.

It was a book on astronomy with great illustrations of the constellations.

"Oh, Dad, you couldn't have chosen anything better!" Jill jumped up and threw her arms around him. "Thanks so much. I see the stars out in the country and often wish I knew more about them. I'll think of you when I use these charts."

It was time to get moving. Dad brought out the turkey and started to rub in seasonings. Mom laid out the ingredients for the dressing. Jill kept an eye on the clock to get the pie out in time and started setting the table. They put on a record of Christmas music in the background.

It felt so good being with her folks again.

"I haven't told you often enough how much I love you," Jill said. "You've been such a support as I went to Teacher's College and started teaching. I appreciate you both."

She gave them each a hug, then they all went back to preparing dinner, each basking in the love expressed. It seemed to warm them.

When the pie was finished baking, Jill set it on the counter. Next, the turkey roaster went into the oven.

For lunch, they had a bowl of soup and a grilled cheese sandwich.

"We don't want to spoil our appetites!" Mom advised.

It was such a happy time. Jill thought that when Dan arrived, the day would be complete. She glanced at her watch. Another hour.

"Guess I should whip the cream for the pie, eh, Mom?"

She took the chilled bowl and beater from the fridge and poured in the whipping cream. Flecks of cream spattered her top as she beat the cream until it thickened. After adding sugar and vanilla, she put the whipped cream back in the fridge. She was ready to garnish her pie.

"I'm going to change for dinner," Jill explained, then headed to her room.

Her cowlick was stubborn and persisted in poking up at the wrong angle. But she was satisfied when she checked herself in the mirror. Her blue sweater brought out the blue in her eyes and matched the long skirt she had bought.

Somehow a long skirt gives me confidence, makes me feel a little elegant.

She headed back to the living room. Her dad gave a low whistle and she preened. *At least Dad likes the outfit.*

Just before four o'clock, she heard the familiar motor.

"Is that the guy we're waiting for?" Dad asked with interest as she got ready to answer the door.

"The very one," Jill said with a smile. "He's here for your approval—as well as mine."

Her mom came into the living room, too, to wait for Dan.

The doorbell rang and Dan came in stamping the snow from his boots and wishing everyone a merry Christmas.

"Dan, this is my mom, Katie, and my dad, Tom." She introduced her parents with a hint of pride in her voice. Dan shook their hands warmly.

Tom stirred up the fire and they sat to visit. Jill was pleased to note the easy way the conversation went between her folks and Dan.

Christmas fragrances filled the room. The turkey was roasting in the oven, the pie was cooling on the counter, and pine was burning in the fireplace. Jill sighed in contentment. So much was familiar from Christmases past, yet so much was new with Dan in her life.

Joanne came bursting into the room, claiming attention.

"I'm back. Hope I'm in time," she announced, taking off her boots.

Before Jill could introduce her sister, she bounced over to Dan.

"You must be Dan," she gushed, appraising him. "You're quite a looker. If Jill ever dumps you, give me a call."

Jill felt her cheeks redden as Joanne winked and left the room.

Dan recovered first. "Quite a contrast in your two daughters, sir," he said to her father. "If you don't mind, I'd like to keep courting Jill."

"With our blessing," her dad responded.

Jill looked at Dan and smiled. She knew her dad approved of their friendship.

Joanne came back in a beautiful red cashmere sweater and a black skirt that reached her knees. She wore black pumps that emphasized her legs, which she carefully crossed as she sat down.

"So, Dan," she began, "tell us about your work."

"Not much to tell. I work as a bookkeeper for a small company. I'm not a chartered accountant, but I'm taking courses. To tell the truth, I enjoy keeping my nose in the books and checking accounts." Dan chuckled and looked at Jill. "Except, now that I've met Jill, the books aren't as interesting as they used to be."

Joanne sniffed slightly. "Well, to each his own. What time is dinner, Mom? Are we nearly ready?"

Her mom jumped up. "I was just about to check."

Jill followed and asked quietly, "Should I offer everyone a pre-dinner drink? Or did you want to save the Coke for dinner?"

"Find out who wants Coke or Ginger Ale with their meal, and who wants tea or coffee with their dessert," her mom said. "Thanks."

Jill went to check, then returned to the kitchen to pour the requested drinks.

"Time to carve the turkey," Mom announced. "Anyone want the job?"

Dan came into the kitchen. "I don't have much experience, but I'll try. My feelings won't be hurt if you give me advice." He smiled as he lifted the turkey from the roaster and placed it gently on the counter.

"Should we let it rest a little before I start carving? That might let me do a better job."

While waiting for the turkey, they set the hot roasted dressing on the table, mashed the potatoes, stirred the gravy, and dished up the peas and carrots. Mom's favorite Jello salad was taken in along with the warmed dinner buns.

"I'd better get busy," Dan announced, picking up the carving knife. It didn't take long to fill a platter of both white and dark meat.

Meanwhile, cranberries, butter, salt, and pepper were put on the table, the candles were lit, and the glasses put in place.

"Everything looks wonderful," Dan commented, taking a seat beside Jill.

He held her hand while Jill's dad asked the blessing. He gave her hand a gentle squeeze at the Amen.

"Would it be okay if I propose a toast?" Dan asked, lifting his glass of Coke. "May the coming year bring health and blessing to the members of this home. Cheers."

He first clinked Jill's glass, then all the others.

"Cheers" echoed around the table before Joanne added, "Dig in."

Jill was proud of the dinner they served and enjoyed the group conversation and the small asides.

When the meal was finished, she rose to help her mom clear the table and stack the dishes for washing.

Once the table was clear, she asked if everyone wanted dessert now or if they wanted to wait awhile.

"Let's have it," her dad voted and Jill went to cut the pie while her mom made coffee.

To Jill's relief, the pie was pronounced excellent. They lingered over their coffee as the candle burned down in the centerpiece.

Finally, her mom announced that she should start the dishes.

"You made the dinner," Dan said firmly. "We'll do the dishes. You and Tom go sit by the fire and relax."

She demurred initially, but she agreed with a grateful smile when Dan insisted. She and Tom headed to the fireplace, Jill and Dan went to the kitchen, and Joanne sat drumming her fingers on the tablecloth.

Jill realized that even doing dishes was fun when Dan was there. They quipped while they worked and soon even the pots and pans were finished. Jill put things away when she knew their place. The rest she left clean on the counter.

When they were finished, they joined Jill's parents at the fireplace to visit a little longer. Joanne wasn't there.

Finally, Dan announced that he had better be going.

"This has been a wonderful Christmas," he said to her parents. "Thanks for having me." He glanced at Jill. "I'm not sure what I would have done if you'd refused to invite me!"

He smiled at them all and turned to get his coat and boots. Jill followed him. They went discreetly behind the coat rack for their Christmas kiss.

"Thanks for a very special Christmas," Dan whispered. "When you wear the locket, think of keeping me in your heart."

"Don't worry about that. You're there firmly."

"Well, if Steve starts to invade, kick him out. Your heart is for me." He kissed her again and left.

Jill turned into the living room, mulling over his closing comment.

What does he mean about Steve invading? I haven't mentioned Steve and Melissa all holiday. Is he really concerned about me letting hatred take hold? I'll need to think this over in private.

She went back into the living room and found her folks getting ready to turn in for bed.

"Beautiful day. Beautiful dinner," she commented.

"Nice guy," her dad said, voicing his approval before settling the fire for the night.

You bet he's nice. Dad approves. I just need to watch getting caught in hatred like Willis Fischer did.

Chapter 43

Jill enjoyed the lunch "date" with her dad on Monday.

Marg West arrived later in the afternoon. Before Jill could even greet her, Marg hugged her, stepped back while waving her hand, and announced her engagement to Joe.

"I'm so excited," Marg said. "We're planning to get married Saturday, July 7. I want you to be my bridesmaid. Joe is asking Dan to be groomsman. I'll never forget that Thanksgiving weekend when we met." Marg paused in her rapid prattle. "Do you think we could do some shopping this week? I would love to pick out my gown and for you to get your dress. There's so much to do. Oh, it's so exciting. You will be my bridesmaid, won't you?"

"Of course, Marg. And yes, let's do some shopping for wedding outfits. Besides shopping for your gown, you'll likely want to start looking for a place to live. Dan surprised me last night by saying he wants to look for an apartment or a basement suite, too. We'll shop for clothes and look for accommodations."

"You didn't tell me you're engaged, too," Marg accused.

"Well, we aren't, but Dan thinks it's time he had his own place. I'm going to help him look. We'll just add Dan's place to yours when we look at places."

Before Marg could answer, Jill's mother came over to welcome her.

"Oh, hello, Mrs. Jackson. I'm just telling Jill about being engaged." Marg waved her ring finger at Mrs. Jackson. "It's so exciting, I can hardly believe it. Joe gave me the ring this morning. I stopped at his place before coming here."

"Well, that is pretty exciting and we wish you the best," Jill's mother commented.

Jill led the way to her bedroom. "Come on. Bring your suitcase and get settled."

When they got to the room, Jill showed her where the towels and extra hangers were.

"Make yourself at home!" Jill said before leaving to join her mother in the kitchen.

"Oh, I forgot to tell you." Marg popped her head out the bedroom door. "Joe is planning to make supper for the four of us."

That said, Marg popped back into the bedroom.

"I guess we won't be here for supper," Jill told her mother. "I hope you haven't planned anything special."

"Nothing that can't wait for another day," her mother answered with a resigned sigh.

"Looks like she's pretty excited," Jill commented as she made tea for herself and her mother. "I guess Dad is having a nap, so we'll let him rest. He seems tired lately."

"Yes, he is. I'm a little concerned, but the doctor has checked him and says he's okay."

They sipped their tea thoughtfully. In the background, they could hear Marg opening and shutting the closet door and running water in the bathroom. The only other sounds were the grandfather clock ticking and chiming, and their china cups clinking as they set them on their saucers.

"This is so peaceful," Jill said. "But it looks like my week is being planned for me. I had hoped to visit Mrs. Brewer and spend time with you and Dad. We'll have to see how we can work it all in with the shopping and everything."

Marg came out and plopped into a chair, heaving a sigh. "There's so much to do. But it's so exciting. Oh, Jill, you're the first one to know. I still haven't called my folks. By the way, can we leave around four-thirty? Joe wants us there a little early. He hasn't cooked for company much and I think he's a little nervous."

"Well, he needn't be nervous," Jill said. "I think it's great that he's doing the dinner."

Marg launched a verbal barrage with events ranging from wedding plans to life in Rosthern, problem students, and more about the wedding.

"You've got your hands full, that's for sure," Jill interjected. She glanced at her mom, who was listening quietly to Marg.

Just then, Jill's dad strolled into the kitchen. "I must have slept," he announced. "Hello, Marg. Been here long?"

"Not long, but long enough to tell everyone here that Joe and I are engaged." She waved her hand at Jill's dad.

"That's nice. All the best to you, I'm sure." With that, Jill's dad headed to the living room.

Her mom suggested a cup of tea, but Marg announced that it was time for them to leave. They walked to the door.

Jill's mom followed them as far as the living room and sat in front of the fire with her husband.

"See you in a bit," Jill called to her parents as they pulled on their winter boots and headed to Marg's car.

Marg started driving before the heat came on. It was cold.

"What's the hold up with Dan?" she queried. "You're such a catch and it's obvious that he's wild about you."

"Who knows what goes on in the man's head?" Jill shrugged. "When he asks, my answer is a yes. But until he asks, I'll wait. I know we both want it to last if we marry."

"So do we. I mean, why would you get married if you didn't think it would last?" Marg pronounced. "It's just that you and Dan seem perfect for each other."

Marg slid her car into a parking space and they got out.

Dan was already there, keeping Joe company.

"What! No hostess gift?" Dan teased as he eyed Jill's empty hands.

"Sorry. I didn't know Joe was a hostess," Jill said, laughing.

Joe was rushing around the kitchen, trying to slap the dishes on the table and find butter for the buns. When he heard the water hissing, he hurried to the stove to lift the spaghetti pot from the burner.

"Cooking for a crowd isn't easy," he moaned as he dished sauce into a pot and put the spaghetti back on the element to simmer.

"Hey, Joe, relax," Dan said. "It's just us. Do you want some help?"

"You could pour drinks, then cut some celery and tomatoes into the lettuce for a salad. Wash that stuff first."

Jill stepped up. "I'll do the salad, if you like. Dan can pour the drinks. I might spill something if I'm as nervous as you are." Jill laughed as she started getting the salad ingredients ready.

After draining the spaghetti and putting the sauce in a bowl, Joe announced with a flourish that everything was ready.

They sat down and Joe asked Dan to pray. He reached for Jill's hand and said the grace, adding a blessing for Joe and Marg's marriage plans.

It was a fun meal. They recounted some of their adventures since Thanksgiving weekend, marveled that so much had happened because of those few days, and generally enjoyed each other's company.

"Do you have time off tomorrow?" Jill asked Dan and Joe.

They both had to work. Dan explained that he needed to do accounts, as there had been a lot of activity over Christmas. Joe had a couple of cars whose owners were anxious to have them back on the road.

"That leaves us to shop," Marg finished happily.

"Do you want to look at apartments or basement suites in the evening?" Jill asked.

"Let's just relax tomorrow," Dan replied. "It's been an exciting weekend."

"In that case, plan to come to our place for dinner tomorrow," Jill invited. "I'm sure Mom would enjoy having us all. We can chat or play games in front of the fire."

Jill and Marg cleared the dishes and prepared to wash them. That took some work, as the sink was full of dishes that were already dirty.

"Looks like a bachelor's place," Marg apologized. "I'm going to have to teach him a few things about the kitchen."

"Good luck," Jill laughed. "I've heard it's pretty hard to change a person after they're married."

"You can't blame me for trying," Marg asserted.

After they were done, they left the clean dishes on the counter, since Marg wasn't sure where Joe would want them put away.

They visited a little longer and then the girls said goodnight.

"See you tomorrow around five, if you can make it by then," Jill said.

The boys stood up and each found their girl to kiss and hold before they went out the door.

Chapter 44

∾

By noon the next day, Jill was tired of shopping for wedding gowns. She suggested lunch, and Marg agreed. It was fun just sitting and talking while they waited. Jill told Marg about Steve Webber and her suspicions. Marg was horrified and wondered what Jill would do.

"Dan says there isn't much I can do without proof. He just told me to keep loving Melissa."

Marg agreed, then went on to talk about her problem student.

"To tell the truth," Marg confessed, "I hope I can soon quit teaching and make a home for Joe and any kids we have."

Jill sighed. "I guess we should soon head home and help Mom make supper. I hope the guys can come by five, and then we can have the evening together."

Later, during supper, Marg told Joe about Jill's problem with the Webbers. Jill flinched. She knew Dan didn't want her dwelling on the situation. From the corner of her eye, she saw him frown.

"The trouble is, Marg, without actual proof, what can she do?" Dan asked. "I'm afraid she's the one who will get hurt if she pursues this."

Marg nodded, but defended Jill's predicament, admiring her concern.

Somehow the topic interrupted the fun they had been having. Jill fervently hoped Dan didn't think she was slipping into hatred for Steve. What would that do to their relationship? She determined to be more careful about sharing her concerns.

The evening perked up after supper and cleanup. They brought out the *crokinole* board and the boys decided to challenge the girls to a game. There was lots of joking, but no high scores. Jill numbed her finger hitting a post. Marg's carom careened entirely off the board as she zapped it in an attempt to eliminate two opposing caroms. Dan and Joe were pretty steady in their aim and were beating the girls when Jill managed to sink a twenty-pointer.

"What's up for tomorrow evening?" Joe wondered. "Marg, did you by any wild chance bring skates along? It sure would be fun to go skating on an outdoor rink. The weather is pretty good, and the forecast is for clear skies—that means stars." He grinned at Marg.

"Oh, nuts," Marg muttered. "I wondered about skates, and then forgot them."

"Not to worry. If we can borrow Joanne's, there's no problem." Jill went to Joanne's room to check with her.

"Sure, take my skates. I wouldn't want to join you anyway," Joanne snipped.

"Thanks, Jo. We'll take care of them," Jill promised and hurried back to the others. "Problem solved. I should have checked the skate size, though. I'll get them and let you try them on."

Jill went back to Joanne.

"They're in the garage. Size eight. You should find them hanging on the wall." Joanne turned back to her book.

Jill rummaged in the garage until she found them. Marg slid her foot in carefully to keep the blade off the floor. Jill could see that they were a little tight, but Marg didn't complain and pronounced them perfect. They all agreed that skating would be fun.

It seemed like they were finished with *crokinole*, so they sauntered into the living room to visit more before the boys left. Jill offered hot chocolate, but no one was hungry after the dinner Jill's mom had prepared.

"Save it for another night," Joe prompted. "Tomorrow night we'll stop somewhere for something hot after skating."

"Tomorrow morning, we're going shopping again. Aren't we, Jill?

Jill agreed, while secretly hoping this shopping expedition would result in a purchase. Shopping definitely wasn't her favorite past-time—even if it was shopping for her friend's wedding gown. She thought it might be more fun if she were shopping for her own gown. Meanwhile, she'd support Marg.

Dan and Joe were soon ready to leave. "We'll pick you both up tomorrow around seven o'clock, okay?" Dan checked.

"Sounds like fun," the girls agreed as they each put their arms around their guy to say goodnight before they left.

Jill's folks had gone to bed so Jill and Marg went to Jill's room to go over the day, make plans, and gab about life in general.

Jill was still worried about Marg's announcement regarding Steve Webber. She told Marg about Dan's concern that she not let hatred for Steve take root.

"I don't really hate him, Marg," Jill said. "I just can't stand what I think he's doing to Melissa. It seems awful that there's nothing I can do but watch and try to pick up the pieces when she arrives at school dejected. I know now that the dejection is from being brokenhearted. I know I love Dan, and I'm sure he loves me, but he seems so obsessed by the possibility that I might let my concern for Melissa turn into hatred for Steve. I'd be the one who ends up heartbroken if anything goes wrong."

Jill punched her pillow and moaned softly at the thought.

Marg gave her a hug. "I can't imagine him being foolish enough to let you go," she encouraged even as the possibility gave her a squeeze in the stomach.

After a while, Marg decided to change the subject.

"Let's turn in and get our beauty sleep. I want to look good when they pick us up for skating," she said.

They soon fell into bed. Marg enjoyed sweet dreams of her coming wedding. Jill's dreams weren't so sweet.

Chapter 45

〜

Wednesday started with shopping plans. After looking at more gowns, the girls would search for Jill's bridesmaid dress. Marg thought she had narrowed her search, which was a decided relief to Jill.

"We'll be back in plenty of time to help with supper, Mom," Jill said as she and Marg prepared to leave. "Dan and Joe aren't coming until seven to take us skating. Is there anything you want us to pick up while we're in town?"

"No, thanks. I think tonight we'll have Christmas dinner leftovers."

"Sounds yummy. How about I pick up Ginger Ale? We should be home in time to chill it."

"Okay. And I hope you girls have luck with your shopping."

Jill added her silent agreement as they headed for the bus stop. Marg was in high humor, waving animatedly as she talked, laughing at almost everything, and generally having a good time. Jill was rather quiet as they boarded the bus. She wondered if she would ever be shopping for a wedding gown instead of a bridesmaid's dress. She was sure that gown shopping would be much more exciting than dress shopping.

They hopped off the bus and headed for the first of several stores. By the time they stopped for lunch, Marg had made the decision for her gown.

"I can get accessories later. Let's shop for your dress after lunch," she offered. "Do you like blue? I think I'd like blue and white for the wedding party. Does that suit you?"

Jill agreed to the color choice and they went for lunch.

After lunch, they spent a couple more hours shopping for Jill's dress, then decided to call it quits for the day.

On the way home, Marg confided, "I never dreamed that by Christmas holidays I'd be planning a wedding. Honestly, Jill, I thought you might be, but I never dreamed it would happen to me."

"I guess that's life," Jill answered. "So far I'm still hoping. I just need to be very careful not to mention how I feel about Steve Webber. To tell the truth, I wish the guy could be castrated, but that's out of my power. I guess that in a way I do hate the man for what he's doing. Dan has warned me a couple of times how hatred can take root and then spill over into other areas. I don't want to hate, but sometimes when I look at sweet little Melissa…" Jill sighed and shrugged her shoulders.

Marg was sympathetic. "You're doing the best you can. Really, Jill, that's a big load. Your problems are a lot harder than the discipline problem I have."

They rode quietly awhile. Finally, Jill pulled the cord to get off the bus.

"I can't forget the Ginger Ale," she explained. "We can walk the rest of the way from here."

Time passed uneventfully until seven o'clock, when Dan and Joe arrived to take them skating.

It was a beautiful, calm evening. The stars were bright and it was a mild night. They could hear the music at the rink before they turned into the parking lot.

"This was a really good idea." Jill smiled at Dan as they took each other's hands to walk to the shelter and put on their skates.

Soon they were at the edge of the ice. Dan put an arm around Jill's waist and they held each other's left hand as they began to glide together. The mellow sounds of "Till I Waltz Again with You" sounded over the intercom, accompanied by some background scratches which no one seemed to mind. The rhythm of the song kept them together.

"We could change the words to 'Till I *skate* again with you,'" Jill chuckled.

Dan squeezed her a little closer. "I can finish that one," he said quietly. "You'll be waiting for my arms."

Jill turned to look at Dan. He seemed so serious. She ended up smiling at him and saying, "Yes, I'll be waiting."

Only, please don't leave me waiting too long. What's the wait for?

They went on gliding around the rink. It wasn't too crowded, so there was lots of room to skate freely. Joe and Marg were just ahead of them. It was apparent that Marg was having trouble in her borrowed skates. Just as Dan and Jill passed them, Marg tripped. She and Joe both hit the ice.

Jill and Dan paused to make sure they were all right. Both Joe and Marg apologized for tripping each other. When they were sure there were no broken bones, they looked at each other sprawled on the ice and started to laugh.

"I've got to admit, Joe, these skates are too tight and my feet hurt. Let's just sit out a few songs and watch the others. Next time, I'll bring my own skates."

Joe helped Marg to her feet and Jill and Dan resumed skating rounds on the rink.

The sky was clear and the stars seemed brighter than usual. It was cold enough to see their breath as they skated, but not cold enough to chill them while they moved. Beyond the rink lights, they could see Christmas decorations still shining.

"What a perfect night to be out," Jill said. "You're a good skater, Dan. I feel more secure skating with you than by myself. I never was very good at sports."

"Glad to help a lady in distress," Dan said as he grinned at her. "Especially when it's a lady I really like to help."

It was the first time either of them had skated that year and they were beginning to tire. Deciding it was time to call it quits for the evening, they glided over to Marg and Joe, who had already taken off their skates. Dan and Jill plopped down on a bench to get ready to leave.

"Ready?" Dan asked a few minutes later. "I guess it's time to crowd into the pickup. She's beginning to seem like part of our group. Maybe it's time to give her a name?"

"How about 'Spinning Jenny,'" Marg suggested. "I think that's the name of a weaving machine. The pickup weaves dreams."

"She's actually rather regal," Jill said. "Maybe we should call her 'Princess.' But she's your truck, Dan. What do you want to call her?"

"I think we'll call her by her color," Dan said. "Just plain 'Red.' So let's go climb into Red, cozy up, and head to a restaurant for hot chocolate. Sorry, no popcorn at the restaurant. That will have to wait until we're at Jill's place."

They climbed into Red. Jill took her customary place snuggled up to Dan, straddling the floor gear shift. Marg slid in next and Joe held onto Marg as he slammed the door shut.

"This is so much fun. It will be hard to go back to work," Marg said. "But July will come and then I'll be here in Saskatoon to stay." She sighed audibly. "I'll try to get back at Easter to finish wedding plans. Let me know if you find a bridesmaid dress by then, or we'll shop for that, too."

"Here we are," Dan announced as he parked outside a restaurant.

After ordering their hot chocolate, Joe found a nickel and popped it into the table jukebox. As the Four Knights belted out "Oh Baby Mine," they were soon all tapping their fingers on the table.

"You know, Joe, with all this talk about what to wear at the wedding, have you decided what color tie you want me to wear?" Dan asked, grinning mischievously at Joe. "I mean, I want to shop in time to get the right thing."

Before Joe could answer, Marg said, "You'll need a blue tie to go with the bridesmaid's dress. A matching hankie in your suit pocket would look really nice. I don't think we want tuxes—do we, Joe? Honestly, we've been so busy thinking about what the girls will wear that we haven't talked about you guys. But I think if you just wear nice suits, it will be great."

Marg looked at Joe to see if he agreed. He just nodded and smiled.

"Maybe tomorrow we could look for a basement suite or apartment, just to get an idea of what it will cost." Marg paused, looking over at Dan. "Dan, I hear you're looking for one, too."

"Well, I've been thinking it's time to get my own place, all right. I'm not in a hurry. Why don't you girls just browse the paper and look at a few places during the day? Then tomorrow evening, if there's something you really want us to see, we could look. Otherwise we could all go to Jill's folks' and play games, listen to music, or just talk. And don't forget, we're having a special dinner at the Bess Saturday for New Year's Eve. We'll see the old year out in real style and celebrate the New Year. It will be dress-up. Warn your folks that you'll be late, Jill. Do you still have a key to your house?"

Jill nodded. "I have one for the holiday week."

They finished their hot chocolates and headed for Red. It seemed too early when they drove up to Jill's house. The guys each helped their gals out of the truck, one on each side. They took their time in the semi-privacy offered by the truck to kiss the girls goodnight before they sauntered up to the door. With another quick kiss, the girls headed in while the boys went back to the truck. Joe was whistling "Oh Baby Mine."

Dan says New Year's Eve is special. He hasn't proposed yet, but maybe he has a ring in his pocket? What in the world is he waiting for? Why can't he make up his mind? We're in love. Why can't we plan our wedding instead of waiting—waiting for what?

Chapter 46

The holidays flew by. Shopping. Talking. Dating. Jill reserved time for a leisurely breakfast with her folks each day. She and Marg took them out for a special lunch. Joanne worked every day and was gone every evening, so they spent no extra time with her.

The highlight of the week was New Year's Eve and their special dinner at the Bess. Jill and Marg dressed carefully and checked each other's hairdos. Jill's dad told them they looked elegant. Jill relished the compliment. Her dad was great and she knew he loved her, but he could be a little sparse with compliments. This was a wonderful way to start the evening.

They sat primed for a good time, but a little nervous. Jill checked the seam on her nylons one last time. She would enjoy the evening no matter whether Dan proposed tonight or left it for the future. She determined not to even think any more about the possibility.

When they heard two vehicles drive up, the girls were puzzled. They hurried to the door when the bell rang.

"Your chariots are waiting, ladies," Dan announced.

"We each brought our own vehicle," Joe explained. "We didn't want to squash you in one vehicle and get your outfits wrinkled."

They all laughed.

Getting into the truck, Jill commented, "It will be kind of fun to be just the two of us for the drive to the Bess. I mean, it'll be fun having us all at the table, but you and I haven't had much time alone this holiday."

Jill slid into the truck seat but avoided straddling the gear shift. It would be a disaster if she snagged her nylons!

"You look terrific. I'm proud to be your escort," Dan said admiringly.

They parked at the Bess and made their way to the dining room. The decorations seemed opulent to Jill. Each table had a linen damask tablecloth and napkins. Cutlery and glasses were arranged with precision. They paused at the dining room entrance, admiring the view while waiting for Joe and Marg.

It didn't take long before all four of them stepped up to the maitre d' to give their names and be escorted to their table. The waiter pulled out the chairs for the girls to sit down.

"I feel like a queen in these elegant surroundings and with all the attention they give," Jill said once they had their menus. "This really is special, Dan. What a super way to end 1955."

They perused the menu, making choices and then changing their minds. There was no rush. Finally they made their decisions and the waiter took their orders. Then they settled back to sip coffee and talk about highlights from the past year as they nibbled on the appetizer and waited for the main course.

Dinner took more than two hours, but they were unforgettable hours. The food was scrumptious and the service was superb. They lingered over the meal, talking and enjoying the romantic background music.

While sitting at the table, they finished making their plans for New Year's Day. They would go to church with Jill's folks. Jill said that her mom planned to have them all over for dinner.

Marg would then leave for Rosthern in the afternoon, providing they didn't have a snowstorm, as forecast. Jill would go back to her teacherage on Monday.

Finally, they decided it was time to leave to watch the fireworks. They strolled back through the hotel, pausing to admire the artwork and Christmas decorations. Then Jill and Dan headed for Red while Marg went with Joe to his vehicle.

Jill snuggled against Dan in the cold pickup. It didn't matter now if she snagged her nylons on the gear shift.

Dan chuckled. "I should take you to a cold vehicle more often!"

"I don't need to freeze in order to snuggle up to you," Jill answered solemnly.

Dan kissed the top of her head and said, "For me, the best part of 1955 was meeting you. You can snuggle any time."

"I'll take you up on that, Mister Dan."

It was close to midnight when they found a good spot to park and watch the fireworks. After the grand finale, they headed back to Jill's folks'.

"No sign yet of Joe," Dan said. "I think he pulled over back a ways to park. We haven't had much time for this and I'm aching to hold you close."

Dan shifted in the seat so his back was to the door and he could face Jill. His arms pulled her close and she responded by circling her arms around his shoulders and kissing him gently on the lips, the cheeks, even the earlobes. Dan hugged her closer and kissed her… gently at first, then more urgently. His fingers found their way beneath her coat and he caressed her breast.

"We don't need to worry about getting carried away in a cold truck," he promised, pausing to restart the engine and get some heat.

Jill was breathless with the excitement and thankful for the security offered by being in the truck and not her living room.

Dan, I love you. I want to have and to hold you from this day forward.

When a pair of headlights pulled up behind them, they reluctantly withdrew from each other's arms.

"Until next time," Dan promised.

Dan and Joe walked the girls to the door, promising to see them the next morning. The door was unlocked, so the girls tiptoed in.

When they got to Jill's room, they wished each other a happy New Year and hurriedly prepared for bed.

It's 1956, Jill thought once she was under her covers. *So much happened last year. I wonder what's ahead for me in the next months until summer holidays! So much could happen at school. And what will happen with Dan? Tonight was splendid. Tomorrow is New Year's Day and the beginning of whatever will come.*

Before she could think anymore, she fell asleep.

Chapter 47

New Year's Day was crisp with blue skies. No sign of a snowstorm. They laughed as they trudged through a skiff of snow on their way to the vehicles, trying to blow warm air circles in the chilly air. Dan and Joe had each brought their pickups to take the girls to church. Jill's folks took their car.

When they came back to the house after church, the tantalizing aroma of roast beef filled the air. While the men sat and visited, the girls helped Jill's mom in the kitchen. Soon the table was set with the best dishes and the food was ready.

"Time to eat," Katie chirped. The men responded quickly.

"Oh, this is so good," Marg raved as she tasted the food on her plate. "I might come to you for lessons after we're married. That is, if you'd take on a student."

Katie was pleased with the compliment and assured her that she would be glad to pass on some cooking tips. "Maybe you'll come too, Jill," she invited.

"You know I could use some help," Jill said. "This summer may be a great time for me to learn something besides teaching skills."

With lots of lighthearted conversation, the meal passed and everyone had their last bite of apple pie. Before long, it was time to wrap things up.

"I've been thinking, Marg," Joe said, "I'm going to follow you up to Rosthern in my truck. That's a light car you're driving and I'm concerned that we may still have that forecasted snowstorm."

"Oh, Joe. It would give me such security to know you're behind me. Thanks so much. I'll put my things together so we can start. I know you won't want to get back here too late—especially if it storms."

Marg was soon out with her suitcase.

"Thanks so much for everything," she said. "It has been so good staying with a family. Next summer, we'll plan to have you over to our place—won't we, Joe?"

Joe nodded agreement as he picked up her suitcase and headed to the door.

"And say goodbye for me to Joanne," Marg added.

"Thanks for the wonderful dinner, Mrs. Jackson," Joe called from the door. "See you all soon."

The door closed behind them.

"It always seems quiet when people leave," Jill commented before starting to pick up the dirty dishes and load them on the counter.

She heard Dan tell her folks to sit and relax. "You made the dinner and we'll clean up," he assured them as he came into the kitchen to help Jill.

"If you decide to go back to the teacherage tonight, it will give you a day to get ready. Besides, I could help you take down the tree and haul it to the fire pit, ready to burn in the spring."

"I've been thinking that would be a good idea," Jill said "When we finish cleaning up, I'll get my things and we can head out, too."

They finished the dishes and Jill went to tell her folks of her decision.

"Whatever you think, dear," her mom said. "It's been good having you, but you're a working gal now."

"I think we might still have a storm, so you're wise to get out there ahead of it," Dad said.

It didn't take long before Jill was packed.

"You're both so dear to me," she said as she brought out her suitcase. Setting it down, she gave them each a kiss and a hug. "You're my 'dear hearts and gentle people.'" She crooned the line from one of her favorite songs. "I'll call you this evening."

With that, Dan took her suitcase and they headed to the door together.

The sky was beginning to look blustery and Jill was glad they were driving back to her place. She settled in beside Dan.

"You look forward to something for weeks, and then it's over," she said, sighing. "But it was a wonderful holiday. I'll think of our New Year's Eve dinner often when I'm warming up soup for supper after school." She giggled. "It's a good thing that I like soup and sandwiches. It's quick. Anyway, I guess I'll keep doing lesson prep at home while the evenings are so long. I just kind of dread walking through that hedge in the dark. But when I'm home, I sometimes work longer than I intend."

"Just make sure that at some point you put it all out of your mind and relax," Dan advised. "Phone me. Listen to the radio—that's why I brought it out. Organize your picture album. But put work out of your mind. And don't think about problem kids—or parents."

"Yes, sir," Jill agreed.

How can I help but think of problems? He doesn't know how attached I've gotten to these kids. I shouldn't, but I keep taking on their problems. Lord, help me not to hate Steve Webber.

"You're quiet," Dan prodded. "Already thinking about school?"

Jill laughed. "Well, it is my job, and I do enjoy it. In a couple years, it will be second nature and not nearly as much work."

"I just want to know that you're not thinking about Steve and what to do—when you can't do anything now."

"Dan, I try not to think of him. When his angry face pops up, I just think of something pleasant and give him the brushoff."

That's true. But sometimes his angry face pops up again and again. I'd love to never think of him again.

Dan squeezed her, pulling her closer. "That's my girl. Think of me instead. Is that pleasant enough?"

"You're the pleasantest thought I can have," Jill answered honestly and dropped her head on his shoulder.

"How about we stop and get a few groceries?" he suggested. "There must be some small stores open today."

The search proved futile. "I should have at least brought bread and milk from Mom's," Jill groaned.

"Not to worry. We're close to my folks. We'll pick up a rescue package there."

Dan drove to his folks and climbed out with Jill following.

He explained the predicament. His mom laughed, then turned to the kitchen, taking a grocery bag with her.

"I'm really embarrassed, Mrs. Fischer," Jill said. "I should have thought ahead."

"Nonsense, Jill. I'm glad you stopped."

Mrs. Fischer bustled around, pouring a pint of milk into a container, putting half a loaf of bread in a bag, and adding a couple of potatoes and carrots.

"That should tide you over, Jill. And here's a piece of cake for good measure."

"That's very kind of you. Thanks. And a very happy new year to you and your husband."

"You can wish me a happy new year to my face," Dan's father pronounced as he limped around the corner.

Jill turned to him and smiled warmly. He looked so unhappy, Jill felt sorry for him. "Well, certainly I'll wish you a good New Year's Day—what's left of it—and a happy year to follow."

Carrying her goodie bag, Jill headed back to the truck.

It didn't take long to reach Jill's place once they were back on the road.

The driveway had been plowed and Dan cruised to the kitchen door. Taking her suitcase, he followed her. Jill carried her groceries and soon had the door unlocked. They both stepped inside.

"Feels a little chilly," Jill commented as she turned up the thermostat. "I'm sure glad I don't have to build a fire to heat this place."

"Let's sit a few minutes and admire the tree before we take it down," Dan suggested. "It really is a good tree."

"You bet. It cheered up my evenings until the holiday came. And getting it was at least half the fun… I can even laugh now about my cookies."

"If that was our only problem, we'd be pretty lucky," Dan said as they prepared to settle onto the couch in front of the tree.

"Want some hot chocolate and popcorn with the view?" Jill offered.

"Sounds like a good idea. I'll make the popcorn while you make the hot chocolate."

They soon sat comfortably with their drinks and popcorn, chatting about holiday highlights.

When they finished, Dan got up. "Time to put this baby to bed," he said as he turned off the tree lights and started taking down decorations. Jill got out a few empty boxes and helped him put ornaments into them.

Dan carried the bare tree outside, then came back in stamping his feet.

"It's starting to snow," he said. "Lock the door. You may be mighty glad for those slices of bread and pint of milk. I'll take off before I'm stranded."

"Please call me when you get home, okay?" she said. "Just to let me know you made it."

Jill gave him an extra hug as she kissed him.

"Thanks so much for bringing me back today."

Dan gave her a hug for the road, then disappeared out the door.

Jill watched until his taillights were out of sight.

Restlessly, she continued staring out the window. The snowflakes were large and piled up quickly.

She tried to pull out some lesson plans, but found herself unable to concentrate.

I wonder what Melissa did over the holidays. Likely her creepy father was there all day.

She pulled out a book, but somehow it didn't get her attention.

Maybe I should heat a can of soup.

She started toward the kitchen when she heard a knock on her door.

Frightened, she called out, "Who is it?"

"Just me—Howard Martins."

Jill opened the door quickly and Howard stepped in, covered with snow.

"We saw that you came back tonight. I'm warning you not to try to go out in this snow. You're a city gal, but we have no street lights out here and a person can lose their direction in a hurry when everything is white. Don't try to go to the school until the storm lets up. If you really have to go over, tie this rope to the rain barrel and hold on for dear life. Then, if you get disoriented, you can follow it back to your house." He paused. "We'll watch that you have heat—we'll see the smoke rising from the chimney. Linda sent some leftovers for you. Now, I've got to get going before it gets any darker. It looks like the snow is going to set in for a while."

Jill thanked Howard profusely for taking the time to come over. He assured her that he would find his way home okay. He had left the yard light on and Linda had turned on lights in the house. The road was still passable, but likely wouldn't be by morning.

When Howard was gone, Jill reached for the phone to tell her folks she was okay. She was informed that traffic in Saskatoon was already being held up by the snowfall. Road graders were out on the streets.

When the phone rang, she reached for it quickly. It was Dan.

"I'm so thankful you're home okay," she said. She told him of Howard's visit. "The people here really seem to care. I'm fortunate to be here for my first year of teaching."

"Take care, sweet Jill," he said. "I'm glad we picked up a few groceries. I'll check with you tomorrow."

Jill went back to open her can of soup, feeling less lonely.

The wind was definitely picking up. She hated the sound of it howling around the corner of the house; it was so mournful.

She looked out the window. There weren't any lights to be seen. Evergreens bent this way and that, shaking off the snow that landed on their branches.

Jill slowly dipped the spoon into her bowl of hot soup and decided she needed a cup of tea to go with the piece of cake Dan's mom had sent. She headed to the tap to fill her kettle.

With a few more sips of soup, she decided that maybe she could find some music on the radio. By the time she had the radio on, the kettle was boiling, so she found a teabag and put it into the pot.

Her supper was finally over, but the storm certainly wasn't. The wind screeched. The snow fell. Somewhere, a dog barked.

"Settle down, Jill," she admonished herself as she ran the water in the sink to wash her few supper dishes. "There's no one out there... you're imagining things."

Just in case, she pulled down all her blinds and checked the lock on her door.

I wonder if the snow is falling as far north as Rosthern? It's good Joe saw Marg home, but I hope he doesn't stay too long. I don't know if he has a candle and blanket in case he gets stuck coming back.

She looked at her watch.

Only eight o'clock. I can't go to bed yet.

She found an old magazine and flipped through some pages. In the distance, she thought she heard a siren but wasn't sure. If it was a siren, it was a long ways off. She was thankful Dan was safely home.

Maybe she'd call Helen Gilmore just to chat, to wish her a happy New Year and get any local news.

She picked up the phone and dialed.

Chapter 48

"Hi, Helen, I'm back. How was your Christmas?"

"Christmas was great," Helen said. "The Christmas Eve service was lovely, but New Year's has been dreadful. First, the snow. Then Stan got a phone call from Mabel Orlick—he's gone to the house now through this snowstorm."

Jill almost held her breath.

What on earth has happened? Helen sounds so upset.

"Are you okay?" she asked.

"Yes. Well, no. Did you hear the siren?" Without waiting for an answer, Helen continued. "It came to pick up Mike Orlick. He was in his room when Mabel went in to ask him if he wanted supper. She found him bleeding quite badly."

Helen stopped to swallow. Jill couldn't imagine what could have happened to a healthy boy like Mike.

"There was a note on his bed, and it said, 'I'm a kid—not a he-man. Stay home and be the man of the house.'"

"You mean he tried to commit suicide?" Jill could hardly believe it. "He was bleeding from cuts he made himself?"

"Yes. Mabel called the ambulance and then called Stan. She was almost hysterical. Stan just went over and I stayed here to handle any calls or messages. If Stan got there in time, he would ride in the ambulance if they had room for both him and Mabel." Helen paused, stifling tears. "Jill, I don't know Mike well, but I never dreamed he was this upset with Oscar being gone so much. He seemed pretty tough."

"I didn't have a clue, either," Jill admitted. "I couldn't decide yet if he was really a tough guy pestering other kids, or if it was a cover-up. I guess it was a cover-up and I totally missed it. I should have guessed. I saw him once with a stray dog that came on the schoolyard. He was so careful with it. He petted it, and even took out a sandwich from his lunchbox. There wasn't a hint of bully or tough guy then. I watched and was quite surprised at this soft side of him." Jill sighed. "If only I'd paid more attention to him."

"I'm going to phone Mabel now… to see if she's home and how she's doing. I'll let you know if they think they got to Mike in time."

"Thanks, Helen. What a start to the New Year! I do hope Mike will be okay and that I'll have another chance with him. I pray he pulls through."

"Me, too."

The click of the phone signaled the end of the conversation.

Jill had to talk to someone. She dialed Dan's place.

"Hello," a gruff voice answered.

"Oh hello, Mr. Fischer. I hope you're having a good year in 1956."

"Couldn't be any worse than last year."

"Well, we'll hope 1956 is better." She decided against asking what had been so bad in 1955. "Is Dan there?"

"If he's not there, he's hanging around here," came the curt reply. "I'll call him."

Dan came on. "Hi, Jill. Sorry I didn't answer."

"Well, I need to talk to you. I have to talk to someone."

"What's up?" Dan asked, sounding surprised.

Jill recounted what Helen had told her. Dan gave a low whistle over the phone.

"This morning we were all having a good time. Man, things can change in a hurry." He paused, then asked, "Jill, did you ever put Mike down in class?"

"No. Never. He was a problem, but I still didn't know if it was orneriness or some cover-up. I hope I never resort to ridiculing a student."

"I didn't think you would. Now, I have to ask if you saw any hint of this coming."

"No clue. I just wish I'd paid more attention."

"Whoa! You didn't ever put him down and you had no clue he could be desperate. I'm telling you, Jill, don't give yourself a guilt trip. You weren't the only person in his life. You've been doing your best with those kids. Keep doing your best and know that even the good Lord has kids who make poor choices. I feel sorry for the family, but especially for his dad. The poor guy is holding down a hard job, and now he'll feel guilty that his work takes him away from home. He probably doesn't like that part of the job already."

"You're right," Jill said. "Oscar Orlick managed to work his schedule so he could be at the Christmas program. That likely took some maneuvering. Thanks for putting it all in perspective. I was sliding into guilt, but now I'll concentrate on the fact that I did the best I could. I'll let you know how things work out for Mike and his folks."

Jill hung up the phone and reached for a pretty teacup. A cup of tea in an attractive cup might help cheer her. The wind was still blowing and the snow was still falling.

She'd curl up on her couch, sip some tea, and hope for good news.

Chapter 49

∿

After midnight, Jill finally got ready for bed. There would be no news tonight.

She shivered as the wind howled, but it appeared that the snow was letting up. She pulled an extra blanket from the box under her bed and hopped under the covers. With her knees curled nearly to her chest, she managed to get one spot warm before gingerly sliding her feet further toward the foot of the bed. Sleep was slow coming, but the cumulative events of the day were tiring. She fell asleep.

She awoke in the morning to a scraping noise outside. Peering through her blinds, she saw Butch shoveling her sidewalk.

Hurrying into her clothes, she opened the door and called, "Hey Butch, come on in here."

Butch came in shifting from one foot to the other.

"What a thoughtful thing to do, shoveling my walk," Jill marveled. "When you're done, can I make you a cup of hot chocolate?"

"Well, Miss Jackson, I'd like that, but I need to get back and help Dad. He's thawing the water trough now for the cattle to drink. The snow really filled in at our place."

"You have all that work at home and yet you came to shovel my walk? Thank you so much. That is really good of you."

Jill went in wondering how she could tactfully show her appreciation. Maybe she could bake a cake or make a casserole. She'd look through her recipes. Meanwhile, maybe she could call Mabel Orlick. After all, Mike was her student and she was concerned.

She found the number and dialed. Mabel Orlick answered.

"Good morning, Mrs. Orlick. This is Jill Jackson," she started. "I'm so sorry about Mike and I'm wondering how he is."

"It's a blessing I went to his room to call him to supper and didn't just call from the kitchen. The ambulance got here in good time in spite of the storm. Rev. Gilmore and I followed the ambulance in his car. They were working on Mike in the ambulance." She suddenly started weeping. "Oh, I can't forgive myself. I had no idea."

"Mrs. Orlick, is Mike pulling through okay?"

"We think so. We think he got to the hospital in time. They gave him blood."

"Mrs. Orlick, I want to share with you something a friend told me when I was feeling guilty for not sensing Mike's depression. When we are sure we've done the best we can with a person, we can't feel guilty when we miss a signal which may be very faint. I'm sure you've done the best you can for Mike. None of us caught any hint of what he was feeling."

"I knew Mike missed his dad," Mabel said. "I tried to get Oscar to take a local trucking job, but he loves the long hauls and the pay is better. We're paying an awful price for higher wages."

Mrs. Orlick sobbed again.

"You can be sure I'll remember you in my prayers," Jill assured her. "When will your husband be home again so you can share the news?"

"He usually phones me his last night on the road. Maybe he'll call tonight and be home tomorrow. I don't know what he'll do when he sees Mike's note."

She sighed and Jill heard the tremble in her voice.

They hung up their phones, each to deal with Mike's desperation as best they could.

Jill walked over to the school to get some materials for lesson plans. The building was cold, so she hurried to pick up her books and return to her warm house.

Bless Butch for shoveling my walk. How would I ever have gotten to the school through the drifts that blew in?

The car was beside her before she noticed it as she walked through the hedge.

"Pretty big load for a little lady to carry, ain't it?"

She looked up to see Steve Webber leering at her through his open car window.

"I'm pretty used to carrying loads like this, thanks," Jill answered with a knot in her stomach.

What's he doing here? How would I ever get into the house and lock the door if he chased me? If I chat, he may think I'm encouraging him to visit. If I don't, he may think I'm angry or stuck-up. Lord, what do I do?

"Thought I'd drop by, seeing as you're here, and tell you Melissa won't be in school tomorrow. Seems she caught a cold over the holiday."

"I'm so sorry," Jill responded sympathetically. "Please tell her we'll miss her and hope she's better soon. Thanks for telling me." She used what she hoped was a polite but dismissive tone and turned to walk to her door.

"In a hurry, are you? That ain't really polite, you know, to just walk off."

Jill's knot tightened. "Well, yes, I'm in a hurry. I couldn't pick up my books yesterday in the storm and I have to plan lessons for the kids tomorrow."

"I can take a hint. Just take care of yourself, miss."

He backed the car onto the road and started driving toward his home. Jill was faint when she reached her door and got inside. She locked it carefully. That man really upset her.

Do I hate him? Dread him? Find his behavior revolting but not the man himself? Dan is so worried about me letting hate grow. Be careful, Jill. Do your best to befriend Melissa. And don't ever be alone with her father… the wretch.

She was only in the house a few minutes when the phone rang.

"Any word on Mike?" she heard Dan ask.

"I talked to his mom," she reported. "She thinks they got him to the hospital in time. It was nip and tuck. She says she wanted her husband to take a job with short hauls in and around Saskatoon, but he likes the long hauls and the higher pay. Of course, she had no idea Mike was depressed by his dad's absence. How was your day, Dan?"

"Okay once I finally got to work. What are you up to?"

"Butch shoveled my walk, so I went over to the school to get some plan books. Then I got a scare coming home. Steve Webber drove up. I hate the way he was leering at me. He told me that Melissa won't be at school and warned me to take care of myself."

"The man is intruding even without school being open yet," Dan commented.

Jill could hear Dan's resentment.

"Dan, I find his behavior ominous. I'll never let myself be alone with him. He gives me the creeps. The way he looks at me scares me. I was terrified just to see him in his car! You can't know how grateful I was to see him back out of the driveway."

"You're right to be careful," Dan answered.

They went on to a new topic, but Jill was troubled at Dan's obvious resentment of any mention of Steve.

Is Dan starting to hate Steve because it involves me? Or is he so hugely concerned that hatred might take root in me? His worry only makes me think of Steve more and how to avoid mentioning him.

"You still there?" Dan's voice called her back to the phone call.

"Yeah. My mind wandered a little. Are you still looking for an apartment?"

"I think I'll settle for a basement suite," he said. "There's more choices. Maybe when I pick you up on Saturday, we can do a little looking. I'd like your opinion."

"Sounds like fun. Meanwhile, I need to find a recipe for a casserole. I need to thank Butch for clearing my walk and I think he often has to cook supper. I'll find a recipe so I know what I need to buy."

"I can't think of anything a boy would rather have than a casserole so he doesn't have to cook. Make it a big one!" Dan's grin was so big she could almost *hear* it over the phone.

"I'll look forward to helping you look for a suite on Saturday," she said. "Tomorrow, it's back to the grind for me. It will seem strange having school and knowing Mike is in the hospital. I'll have the kids make cards to take to him."

"You're a gem. Always thinking of ways to make people happy. I love you, Jill. Lock your doors and be careful."

"See you Saturday. Don't get stuck in a snow bank!" Jill laughed.

"Not if I can help it." Then, with a touch of pride, he added, "Red's pretty sturdy."

They said goodnight and Jill turned to her lessons.

What will this year bring? What will tomorrow bring? How do I help bring something good out of Mike's tragedy?

Chapter 50

Tuesday morning was overcast, which matched Jill's mood as she trudged up the walk to school. As her students started filling the playground with shouted greetings and snow games, however, her spirits lifted. She determined it would be a good day as they began the New Year together. Soon she was ringing the bell to call them in.

After *Oh Canada* and the Lord's Prayer, she told them about Mike. They talked about ways they could show friendship to each other. She asked them if they had any idea why Mike had tried to take his life. Some volunteered ideas.

"We never chose him to be on our team."

"We didn't sit with him at lunch."

"We never went to his house after school."

Jill was surprised at some of the answers. She started to chide herself for not noticing, but then remembered that she had done her best. Ruefully, she admitted to herself that she wasn't as observant as she had thought.

When she asked what they could do for Mike, the answers were to make cards, write notes, tell him they missed him, and visit him when he got home. Jill was proud of them.

"You know, class, if things get bad for you, find someone you trust and talk to them. Remember, we never have the right to take our own lives."

Instead of doing the usual math and reading, they applied themselves to making cards and writing notes to Mike.

Then Jill had an idea.

"Write your names on a piece of paper and I'll collect them." When she had a slip of paper from each student, she said, "Now when I come around, take one name out of the bag. We'll each have the name of a student here today. Draw a picture or write a note to that person. Tell them how they are special or what you like about them."

The students were engrossed in their project and Jill had the opportunity to just sit and watch them. She watched for any clues that might indicate a need for her attention. She missed Melissa and wondered if the girl really had the flu or if the time at home had simply been painful for her.

Thinking about Melissa made her resent Steve even more. *The bully!*

Pulling herself together, she checked the time and dismissed the kids for recess. Taking a break, she poured herself a cup of coffee from her thermos and ate an apple. Glancing out the window, she saw that everyone was having a good time. No problems there.

Before afternoon dismissal, she let the students share highlights of their holiday. It was always interesting to hear of their lives at home.

After the school day ended, Sharon offered to help tidy up. There were still a few things to put away from the Christmas program.

"Doesn't it seem like the program was a long time ago?" Jill asked Sharon.

She agreed.

Butch was busy cleaning ashes from the stove. He commented that the days go fastest when we are busy.

They each finished what they were doing and headed for the door. Jill locked it and turned to thank Butch for the work he had done in the school during the holiday.

"You keep track of your hours, don't you, Butch? When you put in extra time, you write it down and submit your bill—but where do you submit your bill?"

"The school board treasurer pays me," Butch said. "It isn't much, but I'm glad for the chance to earn a little cash."

Jill made a mental note to find out whether Butch's wage was fair or not.

She headed to her kitchen and opened a can of mushroom soup. Slowly stirring in the milk, she hummed a song still in her mind since Christmas. "Joy to the World" always cheered her.

Mike came home Thursday and Jill went with Helen to visit him and take him the cards and letters from the class. He seemed pleased with the attention. Oscar Orlick was sitting beside Mike when Jill and Helen arrived. He looked pale, Jill thought.

There were no other surprises that week.

Jill was glad for the weekend. Dan came out Saturday morning to pick her up. They looked at suites and found one Dan liked on the east end of Saskatoon.

"It will be closer for me to come and visit," Dan said as he hugged her.

They had lunch at their favorite restaurant. Before going home, Jill bought groceries for the coming week. She made sure she had the ingredients to make the casserole for Butch and his dad.

"Are you planning to go to church tomorrow?" Dan asked. "I wouldn't mind hearing Stan Gilmore preach. We could have hamburgers for lunch."

"Sounds great. Yes, I'm going to church. It would be nice to have an escort."

Before they left the store, Jill went back to the meat department to add hamburger to her shopping cart.

On their way home, Jill said, "Isn't it nice to know that the days are getting longer? I can almost imagine it's a little lighter in the evening."

Dan laughed. "I haven't noticed longer days yet, but I'm looking forward to some long evenings at Jill's Cookhouse. That was the name we gave the fire pit, wasn't it? Seems like ages since we sat out there."

They turned up the driveway.

Dan helped Jill carry in the groceries.

"Want a hot chocolate before you go?" Jill offered.

Dan laughed and headed to sit down in the living room. "Have you ever heard me refuse?"

Sipping hot chocolate with their feet up was so comfortable.

"When do you plan to move into the suite?"

"It's time I have my own place," Dan said. "The suite is ready now, so I'll probably give the folks a two-week warning and set out. Now that I've decided, I'm looking forward to moving."

"Well, the teacherage is sometimes quiet, but I still like being on my own," Jill admitted. "I think you will, too."

She slipped closer and Dan put his arm around her shoulder.

"I'll get you to help me arrange things," he said. "I'm better at chopping down a tree than arranging furniture—not that I've ever tried!"

Jill told him it would be fun to help arrange his things. She made a mental note to look for some pictures that would help make the place homey.

It was so relaxing to snuggle and share with Dan. But when he checked his watch, he unwound himself.

"Time to get going," he said. "When should I pick you up tomorrow?"

"Oh, quarter to eleven would be fine. It's a rural church, but they still put on suits for Sunday service."

"I expected that. I'll wear my Christmas tie—and put on a suit to go with it." He gave her a smirk

She walked him to the door.

"What a difference from last night!" she exclaimed when she saw the night sky. "Just look at all the stars."

Dan whistled. "You're really making me aware of the beauty around me. Beauty I somehow missed. Don't ask me how I could have missed something like stars in the sky and sunsets and flowers." He shook his head while he paused to admire the night sky. "On my way, my darling. See you in the morning."

After one last kiss and hug, he walked to his pickup.

Jill watched as he backed out the driveway and turned up the road.

What a contrast. Steve backed out and I was so grateful after the scare he gave me. Now Dan backs out of the same driveway and I'm secure and feeling content about our time together.

Now, let me see. What can we have for lunch besides hamburgers? I think I'm doing well as a new teacher, but I've got lots to learn about stocking my cupboard.

She scanned her shelves a little forlornly. A can of beans caught her eye and she remembered that she had bought carrots.

It's not exactly a Sunday roast beef dinner. Maybe I can still bake a cake for dessert.

She found a quick recipe and set to work. Tomorrow would be a good day.

Chapter 51

Sunday was a bright, sunny day. Dan came to take Jill to church dressed in his suit and new tie. She walked in beside him proudly, aware of some scattered students in the congregation taking covert peeks at the teacher. It seemed like a perfect start to the New Year.

But the New Year didn't continue to be perfect. Somehow, the days took on a certain sameness. There was almost an aloofness, even though Dan continued to phone and come out to see her. They seemed to enjoy their time together, but something was missing. Jill couldn't explain it; she just felt it. In between Dan's visits, Jill spent time with Linda and Helen, grateful for their friendship.

School went well. Mike returned and the students tried harder to include him. But Jill's heart ached for Melissa. When she looked at the girl, Jill's resentment toward Steve grew—especially when Melissa arrived looking withdrawn. She kept searching for ways to stop Steve from abusing Melissa.

Her frustration grew. She realized she wasn't as patient with her students, but she couldn't seem to stop. And she knew she was sometimes showing irritation with Dan.

What's wrong with me? I don't really hate Steve, so it can't be hatred taking root. Maybe it's the uncertainty in my relationship with Dan. Maybe I need a break… I'll plan an Easter holiday.

In the middle of February, Linda took her for a midweek grocery shopping trip. It was her chance to look for the perfect Valentine's Day card for Dan. Valentine's Day was on a Tuesday this year, so it would be a working day for them both, but Dan would be out to see her on Saturday. She'd give him his card then. Maybe they would go for dinner.

The promise of spring was already in the air Saturday morning. Jill had her card signed and ready. Coffee was perking when Dan arrived around the promised time. Jill opened the door and welcomed him, but he seemed a little hesitant. She started to pour the coffee, but he stopped her.

"I need to talk to you, Jill."

He sounded serious, but it didn't sound like a proposal type of seriousness.

Jill sat down to listen.

"Jill, I've told you about my dad. He's not the dad I used to have and love being with. It happened slowly, but it has only gotten worse. I've lived with the results of what hatred and resentment can do."

Jill's stomach started to tighten. This didn't sound good at all.

"I love you, Jill, and I love being with you. But I've watched the Jill I love getting more frustrated, more irritable, and more taken up with how to deal with Steve. I don't think you have room in your heart for both your resentment toward Steve and your love for me. I'm more sorry than you can know, but I can't continue a relationship which is bound for increasing heartache."

Jill sat speechless.

I've sensed him holding back from commitment, but he's wrong. He's wrong. I don't actually hate. I just need a break.

"I've never stopped loving you, Dan. I've hoped to spend my life with you. I've been irritable, but I thought I'd plan an Easter break and get back to being myself."

"My darling Jill, it's not a vacation you need. It's freedom from this load of feeling like you're the only one who can help Melissa and get vengeance on Steve. It is taking root and spreading—as I feared. Keep loving her. But while you realize that her dad is dreadful, accept that right now there is no way you can stop him. You'll end up being a victim of your own hate, and perhaps even a victim of his hate or need for control. Know that I still love you—the girl who was excited and caring and not carrying a heavy load of hatred."

Dan came over and kissed her on the forehead. She reached up to put her arms around him, but he gently stopped her.

Then he was gone.

This time as she watched the taillights dim down the road, it was with a dreadful sense of finality. He didn't intend to be back.

She stared forlornly at her unopened Valentine.

Then resentment toward Dan came.

There was no warning. He could have waited until after Valentine's. No, that would have hurt more. He should have told me I was on thin ice. But no—he talked about his dad. He warned me. Well, he could have at least taken his card. That card tells him how I feel about him.

Then the tears came. Copious, sobbing tears as her dream of a life with Dan was buried. Tears over the phone calls and times with him she would miss. Anger at Steve and what his behavior had cost her. Tears of embarrassment as she would have to admit that she was no longer Dan's girl. Tears even of resentment as her class would soon know that she was on her own.

The tears wouldn't stop. Her throat hurt. Soggy tissues covered the table.

Finally, she got up and washed her face. She needed to talk to someone who would care. She called Helen Gilmore.

Jill tried to keep her voice steady. "Helen, is there any chance you could come over for an hour? I need to talk to someone."

"I'll be right over," Helen replied, sensing something was wrong. "Put the kettle on for tea."

Jill knew that sipping a cup of tea would help. Helen arrived in a few minutes. Taking a look at Jill, she threw her arms around her and waited for Jill to share her problem.

She listened sympathetically and held Jill's hand in friendship. When Jill finished, they sat sipping the lukewarm tea.

Finally, Helen spoke. "Jill, you and Dan seemed so perfect together."

Jill felt herself on the verge of tears again.

"I thought so, too."

"But—I want to say this carefully—I have also sensed a change in you."

Jill looked up quizzically.

"I know your heart is to help Melissa, but I've seen this concern invading your thoughts more often and making you more irritable in general. I love you, Jill, and I appreciate that you called me to share your pain. Let me pray for you now."

Jill nodded and Helen voiced a prayer for Jill to have peace and to be able to give up the resentment which was robbing her of her joy.

Jill felt a little better after Helen left and she thought about what Helen had said.

I mean well, but even Helen has seen a change. I had no idea anyone could see what this situation is doing to me.

Saturday was now empty. She'd call her folks and chat, call Marg and tell her what had happened, and maybe clean house a little.

She started by dialing her folks. Joanne answered.

Just my luck. Now I've got to pass some time talking to her.

Whoa, Jill! You're already irritated with her just because she answered the phone. Maybe you have changed more than you realized.

"Anyone there?" Joanne asked.

"Hi, Joanne. Sorry—I got momentarily distracted here. How are things?"

"Okay. Same old job, same old routine. I think I need to find a place of my own."

"That sounds like fun," Jill said. "There comes a time when we all want our own place."

"Any plans for an Easter holiday?"

"Well, now that you mention it, I wondered about taking a vacation. I just have no place in mind to go to. I guess it will depend some on the weather. I wouldn't be able to go far… still trying to live within my budget. I'm trying to save enough to buy a car."

"A car would give you independence if you're planning to stay out there in the boonies."

"No plans yet," Jill evaded. "Hey, it's good to talk to you. We didn't get much chance during Christmas."

I shouldn't have mentioned Christmas. Christmas was mainly spent with Dan.

"You were pretty busy in your own plans," Joanne answered. "What's happening with you and Dan?"

There it is. What do I say? Can't say "same old."

"We're still friends," Jill said. "He was out this morning."

Well, it's true. He was out. And we're not mad at each other. Just trying to be strangers, I guess.

239

"Anyway," she continued. "Let me know if you find a place of your own. Are Mom or Dad home?"

"Dad's lying down again. He's doing that more these days. Mom's out getting her hair done."

"Tell them I called. I'll try again later. You have a good day."

That was okay. I guess I've rather ignored my family these past few months. I need to do better.

Right now, I'm ready to try eating a sandwich. Maybe I can call Marg tomorrow.

The sandwich tasted a little dry. Jill indulged in a few more tears.

It's like having a death in the family. Tears just come. But it's not a death, and I have to keep going.

She drank some cold leftover tea.

Maybe some music will cheer me.

She looked through her records and found some accordion polka music. But putting on the record just made her think of Dan and the day he'd brought her the record player. The music was cheerful, but it didn't cheer her. Too many memories were associated with it. She soon turned it off and looked outside to check the weather.

It looks nice out. Maybe I'll take a walk. The fresh air will help. I'll concentrate on the signs of spring.

She pulled on her boots and wraps, locked the door, and set out towards Linda's place.

She was always cheered after visiting Linda.

Chapter 52

On Monday morning, Jill gave the kids some quiet work at their desks and sat watching them. So much had changed in her life and plans. She wanted time to really look at her students.

Ivan Kolisnyk was progressing well in English. His hair was still slicked down and his clothes were clean and pressed.

Larry Thompkins looked up at her with a happy smile. Still no running water there… his poor Mom. But Larry was a happy boy.

Honey Wheeler had on a new outfit. She was carefully working on her assignment with an occasional pat to her curly hair.

Melissa Webber was very quiet this morning. What had her weekend been like? Jill decided to walk down the aisle soon, look at Melissa's work, and give her a hug.

Marie Stollery wasn't tattling nearly as much. That was progress. Jill had intended to ask Lois Stollery about Marie's squint for a long time. Now she would do it.

Randy Turner was a little sweetheart in his uncoordinated body. He was a thoughtful boy and Jill appreciated his attention to Ivan.

Sharon Martins was a quick learner and very helpful. It was a delight to have her in class, which was a good thing, since Linda Martins was such a good friend to Jill.

Teresa McNeil was still inquisitive. She'd likely find a way to enquire about Jill's social life—or *lack* of it, now

Mike Orlick was doing well. Jill was grateful he had recuperated and was doing better in his relationships with other classmates. His dad was finding ways to spend more time with him, so some good had come from the near-tragedy. Jill still wondered how she could have missed any hint of depression there.

Butch Taylor was an exceptional boy. He was polite, helpful at the farm with his dad, and dependable as school janitor. She hoped fervently that he could stay in school longer.

After her careful observations, Jill got up and walked down the aisles, noting the work each student was doing. She gave them five more minutes to finish before taking out their math.

During the following weeks, she put extra attention on her work and students. She did her best to put Dan out of her thoughts, but he kept popping into her mind when she least expected him.

I wonder if he still thinks about me? If he has any regrets? Guilt? Loneliness?

She spent more time calling her folks, visiting Linda and Helen, reading, and walking. She enjoyed her walks. The ground was dry now and the trees were producing buds. Some birds were chirping. Days were longer and she loved the soft glow of sunset. She tried not to think how much more fun these walks would be with Dan beside her.

One late Tuesday afternoon as she sat at her desk planning, her thoughts wandered. Her folks were away for a two-week trip. It was mid-March. Easter Sunday was April 1, and she had no holiday plans yet. She sat at her desk, thinking and tapping her fingers. She barely noticed the bouquet of early wild flowers on her desk or the ticking of the classroom clock.

What could she do for Melissa? Suddenly inspired, she took a piece of pretty notepaper and began to write.

> Dear Mr. and Mrs. Webber,
>
> I am planning to decorate the classroom for Easter. Since Melissa is so talented at art, would it be possible for her to stay after school this Thursday? She could spend the night here and then go home as usual on Friday. She would be such a help in making the classroom attractive. Please phone me tonight and let me know if I can plan to have her help.
>
> Thank you.
> Miss Jackson

There. I'll give this to Melissa first thing tomorrow morning. We can work together all evening, and I'll make a special supper for us.

She smiled in anticipation of the surprise for Melissa. Little did she realize that the surprise would be for herself—a very unpleasant surprise.

∾

After supper on Wednesday, the phone rang. Jill hurried to answer. Was it possible that Dan was calling? But the voice on the other end wasn't Dan's.

"Miss Jackson, this is Mr. Webber."

He sounds angry. What could have made him angry about my invitation?

Jill held the receiver a little away from her ear as Steve shouted into the phone.

"What do you mean asking to take a child from her home for the night?"

Jill gasped. "Mr. Webber, I—"

"You are a meddling know-it-all."

Jill heard Melissa in the background.

"Please, Papa."

She heard the smack and thud and knew that Melissa had been hit hard enough to fall.

What in the world have I done to make him so angry? I haven't helped Melissa at all with this idea.

Steve's shouting brought her attention back to the phone call. He was beside himself.

"You need a lesson on minding your own business!" he bellowed. "I have a mind to let you see a man face to face."

"Mr. Webber," she tried again, but there was no appeasing him.

"I'm on my way," he threatened. "I'll teach you to interfere with a man and his family."

She heard the phone slam. Terrified, she bolted the door and pushed the heavy cabinet in front of it. Then she dialed Dan's number.

Three rings.

Where is he? What if he doesn't answer?

"Hello?"

"Oh, Dan, I need your help. I don't know what to do. Mr. Webber is on his way here." She swallowed. "He threatened to teach me a lesson."

"Are you still obsessed with that man?" Dan asked coldly.

"Dan, I can't find my phonebook. Please, call the police for me. I see the dust up the road. He's coming! I don't know what to do. Please, help me. I'm so scared!"

Dan recognized the terror in her voice and realized this was serious.

"Wait until he knocks on the door," he advised. "When you are sure he can't see you, slip out your bedroom window and run for the hedge. Hide behind it. I'm on my way."

She heard the gravel spin as Webber swerved into her yard. She heard the car door slam. In a moment, he was banging on the door.

Snatching up a black sweater, she tried to raise the window. It was stuck. Steve was hammering on the door and shouting. She gave one frantic lift and the window popped open.

She fell out and pulled the window down behind her in case he broke in. Crouching as she ran, she reached the hedge. She flung herself down and pulled the sweater over her body, trying to cover herself a little with fallen leaves to make herself as unobtrusive as possible.

Jill cowered as she heard Steve Webber pounding on the door and shouting, "Let me in! Face a man, if you're so smart. Come out or I'll get you out!"

Can Linda hear him shouting? If she's in her yard, she'll hear and call the police.

The shouting stopped.

Is he circling the house? Lord, don't let him check the yard.

The car door slammed. *Could he be leaving? Oh, let him be leaving. Why don't I hear his motor?*

She felt some hope until she heard the sound of window glass breaking. When he got into the house, he would know she was gone and might come looking.

Oh, Lord, help me. Will Dan come? Will he be in time? Did he get the police? What will Steve do to me if he finds me?

Jill shuddered at the possibility.

She heard another shout from Steve Webber. "There, you interfering know-it-all. That will flush you out."

She raised herself slightly to peer through the hedge and gasped in horror. Smoke billowed and flames leapt from the old house. Jill realized that he had only gone to his car for a can of gas to ignite the flames. He would have killed her, trying to make her come out.

Her terror increased. She pressed herself into the earth, thankful it was dry.

Then she heard it. She was sure of it—a distant siren coming up the road. As it came closer, Steve Webber heard it, too.

Steve cursed loudly. Angrily he shouted into the air, "What are they doing here?"

He jumped into his car, revved the motor, and swung around to head out the gate.

The police were closer now. As Webber turned his car up the road, the police gained speed on him, never stopping for the flaming house.

Jill started sobbing with relief.

She barely heard the sound of metal crumpling and wondered dully if the cook stove had fallen through the burning floor.

I can't save anything. My clothes, snapshots, diaries… my locket from Dan. Everything is gone.

She stayed where she was until the police car turned into the drive. When she knew she was truly safe, she got up from her hiding place. A policeman saw her and approached just as Dan arrived. Both men asked if she was okay as she tried to brush off the dirt and leaves.

Jill explained what had precipitated the incident, although she had no idea what had caused the extreme anger and threats.

"He won't threaten you again, miss," the officer spoke. "He was too angry to be driving that fast on a gravel road. He got caught in a soft ridge, started fishtailing, lost control, and hit a culvert."

Jill stared, trying to comprehend. "He had an accident?"

"A fatal accident, miss."

"You mean he's dead?"

The officer nodded.

Jill could hardly grasp the news. The threats, the fire, the bleak ending… she shuddered when she thought of how different the ending might have been if Steve had caught her.

Then she thought of Melissa and Marcie Webber. She directed the officers so they could take the news to the Webber house and asked the officers to check whether Melissa was hurt.

Now, she felt exhausted. Dan came to her.

"I didn't know who else to call," she said. "I don't know what would have happened if you hadn't called the police." She trembled again.

Linda and Howard pulled into the driveway and came over to them.

"The police were already on their way when I called," Dan explained. "They already had a call from Melissa."

Linda explained her part. "I called the fire department when I saw the smoke, but I see it's too late to save the house."

They stood looking at the smoldering remains of the little house that had been Jill's home.

By now, the police had returned from the Webber's.

"Melissa was bruised, but when I told them what happened, there were no tears. It almost looked like relief. I think that must have been a rather brutal household," the officer concluded. "Now, miss, I need to take a statement from you."

The officer produced his pen and report form.

Jill found it hard to be coherent. She was in shock and feeling tremendous relief that she was still alive. Help had come in time. Her tears were close to the surface.

After she finished describing events to the officer, he thanked her and said he'd call if he needed anything else.

All that was left for her was to wonder where she would spend the night.

Chapter 53

Stan and Helen Gilmore drove in. After greeting the small gathering, Helen said, "Jill, we have an extra room. Why don't you stay with us while everything settles down? You could stay with us until June, if you want."

"Right now, that sounds wonderful," Jill said.

The school board chairman sent word to cancel school for Thursday and Friday to let Jill get over the shock and resettle herself. The kids would need time to adjust, too.

"I can take you shopping tomorrow or pick up some things from your folks," Linda offered.

"I have extras to loan you," Helen volunteered. "You're too tired to go anywhere tonight."

"I can't thank you all enough," Jill said. "Let me know what time you want to go in tomorrow and I'll be ready, Linda."

Dan stood by uncertainly. "I could take you to your folks' place tonight if you want to go."

"I'd like that, but the folks aren't home and I don't have a key anymore. I really appreciate the offer, though. And I can't thank you enough for your help in this mess. It could have been a lot worse. Right now, I'm glad just to be alive."

Dan nodded and added that he was glad, too. He said goodnight to everyone and then hurried for his truck.

Linda said she'd be ready to pick Jill up at nine o'clock in the morning.

"The usual time to start work," she explained with a smile.

Jill left with the Gilmores.

As the day came to a close, she realized everything would be different for the next couple of months. What would come of it all?

When the Gilmores reached home, the phone was ringing. It was Marcie Webber.

"I'd like to have the funeral at the church on Saturday. Could we? I know we haven't attended, but I'd like to have it here in our community. I hope you'll preach, Pastor Gilmore. I've heard that your wife sings, so would you ask her to please sing 'What a Friend We Have in Jesus'? I've always loved that hymn. My favorite scripture is Psalm 23. I would like it if Miss Jackson would read that."

Rev. Stan was a little taken aback. She already had in mind every detail! But he was quick to compose himself.

"Mrs. Webber, you have our sympathy and prayers, and we'll be happy to help you," he said. "Certainly you can have the funeral at the church. I know my wife will sing your favorite hymn at the service. Miss Jackson is here now, so I'll ask her about reading the scripture."

He turned to Jill to repeat the request. Jill quickly agreed.

"We'll ask some of the members to provide a lunch afterward," he said over the phone. "Don't you worry about anything. What time would you like to have the service?" He paused. "Two o'clock sounds fine. We'll plan for that. Someone will pick up you and Melissa around one-thirty, if that will be okay."

When the call was over, he turned to Helen and Jill.

"This certainly has been an eventful evening," he said. "My heart goes out to Marcie Webber and Melissa. I hope we can have a service that gives them help as they adapt. I'll have to check whether Steve had insurance or how the two will survive."

It was getting late.

"Here's some clothes for sleeping and an outfit for tomorrow," Helen said, handing them to Jill. "No offence, but I don't think you want to go shopping in the clothes you have on."

Jill looked at her own clothes and the occasional leaf still clinging to them. In places, dirt was rubbed in.

"Believe it or not, I hadn't noticed." Jill laughed for the first time that evening. "One thing is for sure: I wouldn't want to go shopping like this. Thanks for the loan."

Helen showed Jill her room and the bathroom, then they all said goodnight. Jill headed for a warm shower.

Later, alone in her room, Jill said a prayer for Marcie and Melissa. Then, in spite of all the events, she fell quickly into a sleep of exhaustion.

Chapter 54

Linda was at the Gilmores' door right at nine o'clock, and Jill was ready to go.

"Where do you want to start?" Linda asked. "Do you want to go to the Bay or Eatons?"

"I've got some clothes left at the folks, so I'll just buy some basics. Let's try Eatons first."

Linda grinned. "You're the boss today. Do we need to go by the bank first?"

"Good grief. Of course! Did I leave my brain in the dirt at the hedge?"

They both laughed.

"Speaking of that hedge," Jill said. "It used to bother me some. But last night, it was my hiding place."

Linda nodded in agreement.

By noon, Jill had found a cardigan sweater, two skirts and tops, a pair of shoes, socks, and some necessary unmentionables.

Afterward, they were hungry and found a place for lunch.

"That's my second major change this year," Jill mused as they waited for their order to come. "Things changed with Dan and now things are changed with my living quarters. Thanks for bringing me shopping. I really want to get a car of my own, but it's hard to save enough. Now I'll have to replace more clothes than I'd planned. I'm glad I've got some savings to draw on."

They enjoyed lunch, then headed back to Brentville.

"Thanks again," Jill said as she headed into the Gilmores'— her home for the next few months.

"That didn't take you long," Helen said by way of greeting.

"I just bought enough to tide me over," Jill explained. "I think I'll walk down to the school. At least all my books are there and undamaged. It will do me good to do some planning."

She reached the school before realizing that her key was in the house which was now a charred mess. On the chance that anything had survived the fire, she went down the walk to check.

It appeared that the fire had burned everything. She saw part of some books, but not enough to salvage. Her eye caught a photo album. Reaching for it, she found that some pictures were still recognizable. That was a plus.

Walking around what had been the house, she saw broken dishes, burned pots, and the remains of some canned goods in the former kitchen area. She saw the remains of her furniture in the living room. The records were beyond playing and the record player from Dan was useless. It appeared that books and journals had been destroyed. One stood out a little—another album. She retrieved it and found some pictures she could still use.

She paused and looked carefully in the bedroom area. All her clothes were burnt. The shoes were scorched. Had any jewelry survived the heat? She hoped against hope that the locket would be found. Disappointed, she turned back to the Gilmores' place.

"No key," she explained as she came inside. "Of course it was in the house. Butch has a key, so I'll phone him. We gave him the extra key so he could clean during the Christmas holiday."

She found Butch's number.

"He'll bring it after supper," she announced after hanging up the phone. "He's a fine boy. His dad needs his help a lot at home, so he may have to quit with Grade Eight. It would be such a shame."

Jill turned to go to her room, but first offered to help with supper preparation.

When Helen said she had it all under control, Jill told her that she wanted to spend some time alone reading over Psalm 23.

"Let me know when you want me to come," Jill said as she went to her new room.

Jill started repeating the words of the familiar psalm which she had memorized as a child. This time, she really thought about the words. She pictured herself as the sheep in the psalm with the Good Shepherd providing what she really needed.

I have a place to live until June. Days off to get reoriented. Those are basic needs looked after.

She thought about the next verse: "He maketh me to lie down in green pastures."

I need more time to lie down in peaceful pastures. These next months, I won't be cooking much or cleaning. I can use that time to meditate.

"He leadeth me beside the still waters."

She recalled hearing that sheep couldn't stand rushing water, so the shepherd would dam up a quiet place for them to drink.

My Shepherd doesn't make me do anything I can't handle. I'll hang onto that in the coming days.

She continued thinking on each verse, then paused at "He anointeth my head with oil."

Where did I read that the shepherd checks each sheep for thorns they've picked up during the day? He pulls them out and pours on healing oil. Suddenly the realization dawned. That's it! That's it! I've picked up thorns in my mind and they've festered. The resentments I've hung onto. The hatred

I've allowed to stay and grow. They're like thorns in my mind. Oh, my Good Shepherd, take them out and pour on Your healing oil.

Jill hadn't knelt to pray for a long time, but she knelt that afternoon. She prayed for each person whom she realized she resented or even hated.

She asked for the thorn, as she pictured it, to be removed. She prayed until Helen called her for supper. Jill got up, knowing that her emotions were healing, and went to join the Gilmores.

"Ready for Saturday?" Helen asked.

"Not only for Saturday," Jill replied. "I think I've learned something from Psalm 23 that makes me more ready for all the days to come."

Helen lifted her eyebrows, but Jill added nothing. She needed to spend more time on Psalm 23.

Chapter 55

On Saturday, Jill was ready to walk over to the church early. She found a seat at the front.

People started arriving. Jill noticed that Marcie and Melissa were alone in their pew, so she joined them, holding Melissa's hand.

At two o'clock, Stan Gilmore began the service. When Jill was asked to repeat Psalm 23, she recited it with a clear voice. As she finished the psalm, she continued speaking.

"I've asked Pastor Gilmore if I can make some comments on this psalm. I've known it since childhood, but I never really thought about what it says. While I was preparing for today, I learned something I'd never before realized."

She recounted her experience with the verse about the shepherd anointing the head of his flock after pulling out the thorns they had accumulated.

"Some of you here today may have gathered some thorns during your life, thorns which are infecting your spirit. I'd like to encourage you to let the Good Shepherd remove them. I've learned from experience that hatred only grows, producing no good fruit."

She paused, smiled at Melissa and Marcie, then quietly sat down.

At the conclusion of the service, she hugged Melissa and Marcie, then glanced up at the congregation. She was shocked to see Dan at the back of the church.

She started back to greet him, but people kept stopping her to comment on the fire or on the service. Some asked about her plans. Meanwhile, Dan had started toward his truck.

Much as she wished, Jill couldn't run after him. He was leaving again.

She concentrated on chatting with people who wanted to talk to her. Many had stayed to visit as they ate the lunch prepared by the church ladies. Jill wasn't hungry.

She glanced toward the truck to watch Dan drive away—but he was coming back to the church. She edged toward the back, and Dan came to her. He looked so serious as he took her hand and drew her around the side.

What does that serious look mean this time?

Jill was puzzled. "How did you know that the funeral was today?"

"I didn't. When I saw you Wednesday night, I realized that when I first met you, I thought you were perfect, and that I loved you. I realized that even with what I perceived as imperfection, I still loved you. Then I gave myself a kick in the pants. What a jerk I was to leave you when you were coping with Steve. I should have stood with you and not criticized. I kept comparing your situation with Dad's, but there is no comparison. He's hanging onto his bitterness. You were trying to be rid of yours. I had to admit to myself that if Steve had harmed you in any way, my hatred would have been instant and strong—and here I was cautioning you against letting hatred take root."

Gladys Krueger

He took a deep breath, then continued.

"Today being Saturday, I wanted nothing more than to come out and see you. I brought another locket, hoping you would accept it. If you will, we can put in our pictures. When I saw the cars here, I figured it was the funeral and I came in, certain that I love you. I heard your comments on Psalm 23. I know you have room in your heart for love. What I want and hope and pray is that you can love *me*."

"I've never stopped," Jill said quietly.

"Then will you marry me?" Dan asked intently. "I've known for so long that I love you. I've been a fool not to ask sooner. Please, please say yes."

After all the waiting, all her questions, Jill found Dan's proposal hard to believe, but when she looked into his eyes, she knew he finally wanted what she had desired.

Jill laughed. "I was beginning to think you'd never ask. I've practiced my answer, and it is yes!"

What an incredible ending to the past four days… the terror, the fire, Steve's death—the tumult and uncertainty. And now my greatest dream is coming true!

She threw her arms around Dan. He drew her close, and as they kissed they knew that theirs was a true and faithful love.